Fathers and Sons

First Edition

Published by The Nazca Plains Corporation
Las Vegas, Nevada
2009

ISBN: 978-1-935509-23-3

Published by

The Nazca Plains Corporation ®
4640 Paradise Rd, Suite 141
Las Vegas NV 89109-8000

PUBLISHER'S NOTE
Fathers and Sons is a work of fiction created wholly by *Hank Brooks'*
imagination. All characters are fictional and any resemblance to any persons
living or deceased is purely by accident. No portion of this book reflects any
real person or events.

Cover, Blake Stephens
Art Director, Blake Stephens

DEDICATION

To Leo, who allows me the time to write my stories.

Fathers and Sons

First Edition

Hank Brooks

CHAPTER ONE

Jim Lester had just graduated college and taken the CPA exams. He aced the grueling tests with flying colors, but the State he lived in required that he apprentice himself to another CPA for two years before he could be fully certified and receive his credentials. He had received very lucrative offers from several large firms, all of which he had refused. He wanted to work for a small but growing firm where he could get down and dirty in the trenches. He wanted to experience the full range of accounting, including auditing, taxation and financial consulting. He knew that in a big firm he would be compartmentalized, and perhaps miss out on some aspects of his chosen profession.

When Francie, his fiancée, heard about the offers he was turning down, she really objected to his casual attitude about their future. Poor Jim could not explain to her all the reasons for the choice he was making, but he finally got her to stop badgering him. She was not a happy camper.

One Sunday shortly after graduation, Jim was searching the want ads. He didn't see anything he thought he should pursue. He then turned to the business section. He had noticed that higher end jobs were often advertised there. Bingo! He saw a black bordered ad which read:

"Overburdened, single practitioner seeks an associate for a fast growing practice. Unique opportunity for an ambitious young person. Partnership potential a definite possibility if you are the right one. Fax resume and salary requirement to 602-555-9900"

Jim was really excited. He thought, 'My God. This ad was written to me.' Within minutes, he faxed the necessary documents to the number in the ad. His first impulse was to call Francie, but he decided to wait until after his interview, if he got one.

About 10 AM on Monday morning, Jim's phone rang. Francie was out of town and she said she would call mid morning. Thinking it was she, he answered, "Hi gorgeous, what's cooking?" There was a slight hesitation and then a cheery voice said, "Thanks for the compliment. Do you have a viewing screen on your phone?"

"Oh, I'm so sorry. I thought you were someone else."

"Anyone who calls me gorgeous doesn't have to apologize. I'm Jeanine, Mr. Simmons' secretary. We received your fax, and Mr. Simmons asked me to set up an interview if you are still interested." Without waiting for an answer she asked, "Would tomorrow at 10:00 AM be all right?" Jim's heart gave an extra leap. Trying not to sound too anxious, he said that would be fine. Jeanine then gave him the address, suite number, the name of the practice and finally the telephone number in case there was a problem. Jim in turn gave her his cell number for the same reason.

Francie called almost immediately after Jeanine's call. As he had promised himself, he refrained from telling her about his interview. Francie was a buyer for Bloomingdale's and was currently in Los Angeles on a buying spree. She told him that she would be gone for at least another three weeks, but would be home for two weeks upon her return. During the conversation, he thought about having sex with Francie and by the time she hung up he was as hard as a nail. I'll have to do something about this, he thought, and undressed quickly, got into bed and masturbated slowly and sensuously. His mind wandered to his brother's high school friend, Mike. He began to fantasize that he and Mike were playing a hot game of 69. Then Mike was fucking him. Then he was fucking Mike. He kept fantasizing about Mike, until his chest was covered with cum. It never even occurred to him that his fantasy was homosexual or that Francie wasn't even close to being his masturbation fantasy.

On Tuesday morning Jim dressed in his only good navy blue suit, white shirt, sensible tie, black knee length socks, and dress black shoes. He checked himself out in the mirror, admired how business like he looked and headed out the door to meet Jeffrey Simmons, CPA.

When he arrived at the office in downtown Phoenix, a young man was leaving the office. Jim wondered if he was another candidate for the position. He presented himself to the receptionist, and couldn't help but tell Jeanine that she was indeed gorgeous and his greeting yesterday would hold. As far as she was concerned he was hired. She knocked on Mr. Simmons' door and he said to come in. She ushered Jim into the office and introduced the two men. They shook hands warmly, each admiring the other's firm grip.

The moment Jim saw Jeff, he was thunderstruck. Here was the handsomest man Jim had ever seen. Jeff was about five years older than he, and an inch taller at about 6'1". He was built like a football player, and obviously worked out. He was wearing a sport shirt and Jim could clearly see soft, furry hair on a well developed chest. He felt an engorgement in his penis and sat down as quickly as possible in order to hide it. This had never happened to him before, at least not with a man. He realized that he was turned on by Jeff Simmons and now he was so confused, he wondered how he could get through the interview. He also could see why Jeff was so successful.

Jeff too was shocked at his reaction to meeting Jim. Grasping Jim's hand, he felt his boxer shorts being stretched, and he sat down quickly. This was just not right. He was a heterosexual, married man. He had never been aroused by a man before. But what a man! Jeff thought that Jim was the handsomest man he had ever seen. He wasn't really muscular, but he was lean and hard. Jeff guessed that Jim's sport in college had been track. He tried to knock the sexual thoughts he was having right out of his head, and get on with the interview, but he felt the room spinning. This was going to be hard, he thought, and I can't understand any of what is going on.

Jim spotted the picture of a beautiful young woman on Jeff's desk. When Jeff caught Jim looking at the picture, he was roused from his reveries. He explained that the picture was that of his wife, Marie. Jim's stomach sank and he felt disappointment. He wondered why. This is crazy. Why should I care that he's married? After all, I'm engaged and I AM STRAIGHT. In spite of that, Jim kept shifting in his seat to undo the discomfort he felt from his ever bulging package. He couldn't help notice that Jeff was doing the same thing.

The interview was a non interview to say the least. The two men felt so comfortable with each other. They had gone to the same college and they compared notes on their college days, especially, sports, booze and women. They talked about the local sports teams, the social life their city, Phoenix, afforded, about their families and dozens of other things. The time passed so quickly that they felt like two old friends who hadn't seen each other in ages. Finally, they discussed salary and Jeff said he'd like Jim to start the following Monday. They shook hands on it. Jeff buzzed Jeanine and told her to cancel all the other interviews. The job was filled. Jeanine was ecstatic. Suddenly Jim caught Jeff checking out his watch and thought it was time for him to leave. Instead Jeff asked if he would like to have lunch with him. Jim said that would be great. Neither had realized that they had been talking for more than two hours.

They went to a little café just around the corner from the office. Now indeed they could talk like old friends. Jim volunteered that his fiancée was away more than she was home and how frustrating it was. To which Jeff grinned and said, "I bet you use your hand a lot."

"You know it." Jim replied.

Now it was Jeff's turn. My wife is a correspondent for UPI and she's overseas at least 80% of the time. Now you know why I asked about hand action. Then he said something only two old friends would talk about. "I think she's having an affair with her photographer. She's asked for a divorce."

"Oh, I'm sorry." Jim replied.

"No need to be sorry. It's for the best.

"What's he look like? The photographer, I mean." Jim asked curiously. Jeff was so handsome he just couldn't imagine what she could see in another man. Jeff had been sitting across the table from Jim. Now he got up and scooted to the chair next to Jim so that they were sitting at right angles. Jeff's knee touched Jim's. Electricity shot up Jim's spine, but he didn't move.

"He," Jim began in a whisper, "looks more like a Lynne. Marie's photographer is a woman."

Jim was speechless. All he could manage was a "WOW!"

"It explains why she was so frigid with me. As for me, I'm working on moving on. Thank God there are no children. Hey," Jeff said. "Our women are both away so why not have dinner with me tonight. Don't take this wrong but I feel so connected with you. I enjoy your company so much. Please say yes."

"OK. Sure." Jim hoped he didn't sound too anxious.

"That's great. Look, after work, I want to go home, shower and change. Wear something casual tonight and come by about 6:30. I live in that high rise just one block up." Jeff pointed to the building, and gave Jim his apartment number, telephone number and cell number. He was making sure that they would have dinner together that evening. He just couldn't bear to say goodbye to this handsome hunk. He was definitely ashamed of his feelings, but he was determined to pursue them and see where they led.

Then, as if a light went on in his brain, he said to Jim. "I've got a better idea. Why don't you come back with me? I'll show you to your office, give you a couple of clients' files I want you to take over, and you can start orienting yourself to our routines. Jeanine will give you some guidance. Then you can come home with me and shower there. You're only slightly shorter than I am and I can lend you some casual clothes to hang out in. Then he added quickly. I'll put you on the payroll immediately, of course."

"Of course," Jim replied. Then the two laughed heartily.

Jeff showed Jim to his office and Jeanine got him some vital supplies which she placed in a storage closet in the room. The desk already had a calculator and a computer which she said was networked with all the other computers in the office. Jim booted up, and she told him that every computer in the office had the same password, "Simmons." As the computer was booting up, Jeanine explained that Jeff wore a shirt and tie when he went to a client, but in the office a sport shirt and slacks would be fine. When clients came to the office they knew what the dress code was and it was fine with them. She advised him to keep a clean shirt and tie in his office in case he had to run out to a client. Then she brought him the files Jeff wanted him to start on, and left him to review them and write down any questions he might have. All the while, Jeff was in his office answering the messages he had received during the morning he spent with Jim. Both their doors were open and Jim could here Jeff laughing, but at the same time giving some sound business advice, and saying things like yes, I'll be there on Thursday. It was plain to Jim that Jeff enjoyed a terrific relationship with his clients and much respect.

Jim was struck immediately by how well organized and professional the files were. All the work papers were well documented and there were ample audit trails. He could see that both clients were due for quarterly reviews. Based on the previous work papers, he made notes on which areas he particularly wanted to look into at the next review.

"How's it going?" Jim looked up to see Jeff at his door.

"Great. I see I need to make some appointments. Do I do it or does Jeanine?"

"You'll do it in the future, but for now, Jeanine has scheduled you next Monday and Tuesday at Badger Manufacturing and Wednesday and Thursday at Royal Emporium. You can work in the office on Friday preparing interim financial statements and organizing their files. I'll go with you the first morning at each job and introduce you. Then I'll leave, but if you have questions call me on my cell phone. If you know I'm at the office, you can call me here. Now, have you any idea what time it is? Jeanine has been gone almost an hour."

Jim looked at his watch. He couldn't believe that it was 6:30. He was about to go home with Jeff. His heart started to beat wildly and he felt throbbing in his groin. This is crazy, he thought. Stop this. You are engaged to be married. You are not supposed to feel this way.

Since Jim had come down town by bus and Jeff had walked to work, there were no vehicles to worry about and they started their short walk to Jeff's apartment.

When they entered the apartment it was obvious that a woman had decorated. It was very frilly and did not reflect Jeff at all. "Let's see what I can give you to wear tonight. I have a restaurant in mind and a nice cocktail lounge afterwards where we can really get to know each other well." Jeff went to his closet, and got out a casual pair of slacks that he knew were slightly short on him and then chose a complementary sport shirt and laid them neatly on his bed. Next he went to his dresser and took out a pair of boxer shorts and a pair of socks. Jim's own socks and shoes would continue to do nicely. "That should work well," he said.

With Jim still in the bedroom, Jeff started to undress. He folded his slacks neatly and hung them in the closet. Then before Jim knew what happened, Jeff had stripped completely and thrown everything into a hamper in the bathroom. "What are you waiting for? He asked. Let's shower together and we can do each other's backs." Jim stood stunned. His tool was standing too, and he knew he couldn't get undressed this way. "You shower with men at the gym, don't you?" Jeff added with a leer.

Too shocked to move, but not turned off, Jim finally looked at Jeff. Up until now, while Jeff was stripping, he had avoided staring at him. Jeff looked like a Greek statue. He had short, curly black hair. His chest was rippled with muscles. His nipples were tan and rather large. He had soft furry black hair on his chest. His biceps were enormous. His pubic hair was definitely trimmed. Jeff's penis was erect and Jim was sure he could see precum on the tip. It was at least eight inches, cut, and wider than Jim's, but Jim was sure his was longer.

Jim realized he had two choices. He could bolt and run and say sayonara to the job, or he could soap his boss's back. In a second his choice was made, and he was naked. Jeff was adjusting the water temperature in the shower, still sporting a boner. Jim noted that the shower was wide enough that they could avoid touching each other, but Jeff had other ideas. Once in the shower, he found reasons to reach across Jim's body to get the soap and replace it on the tray, to adjust the water temperature over and over, etc. More than once their penises brushed each other lightly. Jim was heady. He thought he was going to faint. He had never in his life thought about another man, and now all he could think about was taking Jeff's tool into every opening in his body. He wanted Jeff's juice down his throat and up his ass. This was insanity. He had never, ever had thoughts like this. He had nothing against gays, but he had often made fun of them. Jim was going crazy. His head was spinning. He was simply spaced out, and without realizing it, he slumped against Jeff, who grabbed him and held him up.

"I know." Jeff said. I feel the same way. The moment you walked into the office, I wanted you. I have never wanted another man in my life. What's happening here? I'm going crazy and you're making me that way." As the older of the two, Jeff felt he needed to take the lead and do something very quickly. With that he embraced Jim strongly and pressed his lips to the younger man. Instinctively, Jim's lips parted and their tongues began a dueling match. Their hands wrapped around their throbbing tools and they began massaging each other with their precum. "Please stop," Jim pleaded. "I don't want to cum yet. Let's get good and clean and take this to the bedroom."

Jeff released his new lover. They washed each other's backs and paid particular attention to the love holes they knew would be filled that night. Eventually they exited the shower, reluctant to let go of each other. As neat as they had been before, they unceremoniously tossed the neatly laid clothes off the bed and made love to each other.

How they knew, neither could tell you, but instinctively they both knew what to do and how to please the other. They got into a 69 position and for the first time they each took a penis into their mouths. There was no hesitation. This was thrilling and each marveled at how good the other tasted. Then before they could cum, Jeff released himself. He took some condoms and some lube from his night stand. Patiently, he got Jim ready with his well lubed fingers. First he inserted one finger into Jim's love hole, then two and even three. Then with Jim on his back, so they could kiss while they fucked, Jeff drove home. Initially it hurt, but Jim didn't care. Once past the sphincter, Jeff's cock began to massage Jim's prostate, and it was heaven for both of them. They were both moaning softly at first, but then their breaths shortened, the moaning increased. Jim gyrated and thrust to meet Jeff's incessant rhythm. They came almost simultaneously, Jeff in the condom and Jim all over his chest. Jeff collapsed on Jim's body, spreading Jim's cum all over both of them.

Out of curiosity, Jeff put some of Jim's cum on his finger and tasted it. He liked how it warmed his mouth and the salty taste, so Jim did the same. With cum in both their mouths, they kissed passionately. They lay still for a while until Jim said, "I'm hard again. It's my turn."

There was no dinner that night and the two men made love for hours until they finally fell asleep in each other's arms.

CHAPTER 2

Jim awoke at about 3 AM. He could hear Jeff breathing very lightly at the other end of the bed. Their bodies were at least a foot apart. Jim reflected on the events of the evening and marveled that he had had sex with a man. He believed that he should feel disgusted. He believed that he should want to slug Jeff in the eye, and tell Jeff what an asshole he was for having lured him into this predicament. Strangely, he felt none of those things. He wanted rather to scoot over and pull Jeff into his arms, and make endless love to him again. He still could not accept the fact that he might be gay. He only knew that he had fallen hopelessly in love with a dude, AND HE DIDN'T CARE.

He had to pee badly, so he got out of bed as quietly as he could and headed for the bathroom. He had familiarized himself with the layout of the bedroom and bathroom that evening and so he went to do his business in the near darkness.

Jeff had not been able to sleep at all and was only pretending so as not to disturb Jim. When Jim got out of the bed, Jeff panicked. He was sure Jim would quietly slip on his clothes and leave. Jeff shivered thinking Jim might be out of his life forever. The mere fact that he didn't use a light in the bathroom surely meant he was going to leave on the sly and Jeff couldn't blame him. Tears began to roll down Jeff's cheek. He chided himself on having been too aggressive. He should have let their friendship mature and then grow into love. But he himself had fallen in love instantly and he couldn't help luring Jim into sex. Fool! Fool! Fool! And worse yet, sex with a guy, a dude. What madness. 'I must be out of my mind,' he thought.

And then a miracle occurred. Or at least, it was a miracle to Jeff. Jim climbed back into bed. Not only did he climb back into bed but he hunkered up to Jeff, who was facing away from him, and nested against him like 2 spoons in a drawer. Jim's erect cock did some nesting also, right up against Jeff's crack. That did it. Jeff lost it. He began to sob uncontrollably. Now it was Jim's turn to panic. He was sure that it was straight Jeff who was disgusted and wanted him out as soon as possible. It took all his strength to ask Jeff if he wanted him to leave.

Jeff's sobs changed to gales of laughter. "I'll fire you if you do." he giggled. "Oh Jim, I can't explain it any more than you can, but don't you see how helplessly in love with you I am?" Now it was Jim's turn to giggle.

"Do you know how ridiculous that sounds? Jim said. "You love a dude. I love a dude. How can it be?"

"I told you. Don't try to make sense of it." Jeff replied. "I'll tell you one better." he added. "I wouldn't be embarrassed to advertise it in the newspaper."

"Well that might be a good idea because I can't think of a better way to tell Francie and my folks than through an ad in the paper. And you've got Marie and your folks to think about. Do you perchance have any thoughts on how you're going to explain me, and how I'm going to explain you?"

Jeff rolled over, pulling Jim fully against him. "Tell you what," he said, "I'll worry about it tomorrow. After all, tomorrow is another day." That having been said, he scooted down and took Jim's very hard cock into his eager mouth. Jim was finished being cute and coy. He placed his hands on the back of Jeff's head and pushed himself deeper inside Jeff's mouth. Jeff resisted gagging as he swallowed Jim's engorged head. All he could think about was that he was deep throating the love of his life, and nothing else mattered. His tongue ran sensuously up and down Jim's shaft. Jim was moaning and squirming and pushing harder and harder into Jeff's mouth. It didn't take him long to cum. With one glorious scream he shot streams and streams of his precious fluid into Jeff's eager mouth. Jeff withdrew somewhat so that he could taste and capture Jim's love juice. After they caught their breaths, Jeff was kind enough to share Jim's cum with him via some serious kissing. Then they dozed off again.

Needless to say they overslept. Jeff called the office and informed Jeanine that he would be a little late. He didn't mention Jim because technically Jeanine didn't expect him to start until the following Monday. That thought gave Jeff an idea. "Would you like to take the rest of the week off so we don't have to explain why we are both late together."

Jim considered the offer for an instant and then replied, "Absolutely not! First of all, I am so ready to get going at work, and you could really use my help. Secondly, since you are ready to place an ad in the paper, why not be open with Jeanine and see what kind of reaction we get."

"Hey babe, what a great idea."

The word, babe, did not escape Jim's computer brain. Yesterday, if some guy had called him "babe," he would have socked him in the eye. Today, coming from Jeff, it sounded like a chorus of angels.

"You'll be happy to learn, BABE, that your lowly employee is always full of good ideas." Jeff caught the irony in Jim's tone and grinned so disarmingly that Jim added, "Like right now, I think we should get back to bed and start where we left off."

"No way, HON," Jeff replied giggling. "We'll never get to the office. You shower while I fix us breakfast. Wear the clothes I laid out last night. It'll be fine for the office. Yell when you are done and I'll shower, shave etc. Wow, I forgot." He went into the bathroom, and somehow found a new toothbrush and razor and gave it to Jim.

"You know what would be real nice, babe? When you're through, put the razor and toothbrush next to mine." Jim smiled very broadly and Jeff's heart melted into mush.

They finally arrived at the office at about 10 AM. On the way over, they made a pact that they would never let their love and private lives interfere with business. They never did break that rule.

Jeanine was very surprised that Jim arrived with Jeff, but for the moment decided not to say anything. She handed Jeff several phone messages and went back to her typing.

"Before I answer these calls, let me give you some stuff to work on." Jeff beckoned Jim to follow him into his office. When he opened the door, Jeff motioned to Jim to enter first. Then making sure that Jeanine could see, he gave Jim a whack on the rump as Jim passed in front of him. When they were both inside, Jeff left the door open and whispered to Jim, "That should start her thinking." He then went over some files with Jim. In every case some adjusting entries were required and then financial statements needed to be prepared. One account was on a year end extension. In addition to completing the work and financial statements, Jim would need to prepare tax returns as well. Given his inexperience, he reckoned he would need until close of business on Friday to complete the work. He also figured that Jeff had figured that out himself.

Jim took the files into his office and put them in neat piles on a cabinet in his office, deciding to do the year end client last. No sooner was he inside than Jeanine came in and closed the door. "Jeff will be on the phone for a while. Now I'm not exactly blind and I wasn't born yesterday. What the hell is going on with you two? And if it's what I think, I want you to know I totally approve. Jeff needs someone better than that bitch he's soon to be divorced from. There I said it."

Jim was learning that Jeanine often ran on before anyone could respond to her, but she was never offensive. Jim decided to be light hearted and in his best southern belle accent he said, "Why dahlin'. Whatever do you mean?

"Look Jeanine," he then got serious. "Jeff said that if you asked any questions or noticed anything different, you should ask him about it. OK?"

"Deal!" She responded, and left Jim's office so he could get to work.

Jim was so enjoying his work and got so immersed in it, that he actually forgot about the sex of last night and the sex yet to come. But occasionally his mind wandered to thoughts of Jeff and his magnificent body. In those brief moments it became necessary for him to adjust his own boxers.

"A good accountant is always at a good stopping point." Jim heard Jeff announce from Jim's door. "It's time for lunch. Let's go."

"Okay," Jim answered "but today's lunch is on me. I don't want to feel 'kept.'" Jeff understood and nodded in agreement. On the way to the restaurant Jim said that he needed to go home that evening. He wanted to check his mail, phone messages and pick up some clean clothes for work. Then, with a smile on his face, he said to Jeff, "It sure would be nice if you were to go home with me."

"The pleasure will be mine." Jeff really wanted to see what Jim's place looked like.

As soon as Jeanine left for the day, Jeff and Jim reverted to two high school kids. They romped around the office trying to grab ass each other. Then they literally ran over to Jeff's apartment. They went up to the apartment and Jeff packed an overnight bag and clothes for work the next day.

"Are you thinking you might get lucky tonight?" Jim quipped, and they both laughed. Then they went down to the underground parking garage to get Jeff's car. When they reached the car, Jim said, "I'm shocked. I was expecting a Benz or a Beemer at the least, certainly not a Saturn."

A little chagrined, Jeff retorted. "It's a great car, it's economical, and it gets me where I need to go."

This really upset Jim and he quickly apologized. Then with a grin he asked, "Does that represent our first lover's quarrel?" Jeff smiled, and grabbed Jim in a hug. Reluctantly they released each other and they started out to Jim's apartment.

In the car they drove in relative silence, both lost in their own thoughts. They did briefly discuss where to have dinner. Jim said that he had plenty of food and he would throw something together. The only other interruption to the quiet was Jim's voice occasionally giving Jeff directions to his apartment.

Suddenly Jim dropped a bombshell. "Jeff, I've been thinking," he began. "How can two guys who have been straight all their lives, who never touched another guy, especially not 'there,' how can they both become gay in an instant? It makes me wonder a couple of things. Am I just queer for you and maybe no other man could arouse me? Were there ever events in my life which should have given me some warning that I might be gay?" Jim turned to Jeff, who was staring straight ahead at the road. "Jeff," he said, "I've thought about a couple of times when maybe I should have been alerted."

Still concentrating on the driving and without turning his head, Jeff reached over and put his palm on Jim's crotch. Jim sighed and slumped in his seat a little to help Jeff out.

Jeff turned to Jim for a second and said, "Honey, there is no doubt in my mind that we are soul mates. I have been dwelling on the same two questions, and I have some answers too. Let's share the info when we get to your place.

CHAPTER 3

Jim directed Jeff into the parking area of his condominium complex. Then he directed him to the guest parking area. Jeff was surprised at how high end the complex was. It consisted of three, ten story buildings and Jeff figured there must be twelve apartments on each floor. He wondered how a young, recent graduate could afford such luxury, but remembering the incident with his car, he decided not to say anything. By this time, however, the soul mates were reading each other's minds.

"The apartment belongs to Francie." Jim explained. "Her parents are well off and gave it to her as a graduation present two years ago. If you are doing the math, she's not older than I am. She's just a genius who graduated two years before me.

Jeff found a free guest space and parked. He removed his overnight bag and his clothes for tomorrow, which were hung neatly on a hangar. Jim led him to the middle building. Each building had a telephone security system. Visitors had to be buzzed in, but Jim had a key, of course. They entered a beautiful lobby, full of artificial plants, easy chairs, sofas, and marble tables. Jeff wondered if anyone ever used it. Then his question was answered. On the way to the elevator he saw a diminutive, elderly lady sitting in a winged back chair which seemed to absorb her total body.

"Good evening, Mrs. Crane," Jim said cordially to the old lady.

"Hello, Jimmie," she replied. "I'm waiting for my son to pick me up. He's taking me out to dinner tonight for my birthday."

"Happy birthday." both men said in unison, and Mrs. Crane smiled back at them.

Jim rang for the elevator and the door opened immediately. "Have a good time." he said to Mrs. Crane as the door closed behind them. Oblivious to the security camera, as soon as the door closed, Jim threw his arms around Jeff and began to kiss him with insatiable yearning. Jeff dropped his bag. He was still holding the hangar with his clothes, and with his free hand he returned Jim's hugs. This is going to be a good evening, both men thought.

The elevator took them to the top floor and still Jeff made no comment. He knew that the cost of a condominium increased with elevation. Jim led them to his apartment, fumbled for his key and let them in. They stood in a narrow hallway, and kissed again. Jim took Jeff's bag, led him to the bedroom and laid the bag at the foot of the bed. Then he took the hangar and hung Jeff's clothes in his closet. "Look." he said to Jeff, "Our clothes are hanging side by side."

"You're a fucking romantic." Jeff said. With both their hands now free they hugged each other and kissed. Their tongues found each other and dueled madly. Their cocks ground fiercely against each other. Jim finally broke away.

"Later, my love," Jim said. We need to have a bite to eat and we have lots to talk about. He started for the kitchen and Jeff followed, taking in the whole apartment. The bedroom was adequate, about 12 x 12 with a bathroom. There were two doors in the entrance hallway, one to the right and one to the left. The one to the left led to a small bedroom about 8 x8. It was nicely furnished as an office, with a writing desk and a computer desk. Each desk had a chair of its own. There was a fax/answering machine on the writing desk. Wherever there was available wall space, there were well filled book cases. The door to the right led to a small powder room. The living room and dining room were one great room. Even though the kitchen was a small working kitchen, the great room made the apartment look huge. There was a balcony about 12 x 6 off the living room behind sliding glass doors. The balcony afforded a lovely view of the city. On the other side of the living room, a small hallway led to the master bedroom.

Jim investigated the contents of the refrigerator and announced that he had the fixings for onion omelets, and he could defrost a couple of bagels, if that was OK with Jeff.

"That's perfect." Jeff said. Instinctively, he went to a cabinet where he found everything necessary to set the dining room table as Jim began work on the omelets. It was amazing how well they worked together, in the office, in the house and certainly in the bedroom.

"One more thing," Jim said. "Put out two wine glasses, and you'll find some Chardonnay in the fridge. Jeff did as he was told, and then turned toward Jim. Jim was facing the stove and was almost done with the cooking. The omelet was browning and the bagels were in the toaster. Just as Jim pushed down the lever on the toaster, Jeff came up behind him. He kissed Jim on the back of his neck. Then he enveloped Jim's waist and let his hands wander down to Jim's ever bulging package.

"You've got a one track mind," Jim complained, "and how I love it. Sit down now." he commanded. He ladled half the omelet on one dinner plate and the other half on another. He brought both plates to the table and then got a ketchup bottle out of a cabinet. The toaster popped, and he put all four bagel slices on a dish. He took the butter from the fridge and placed it on the table as well. When everything was out, he finally sat down, lifted the wine glass Jeff had filled and said, "Here's to us, now and forever." They each took a sip and Jeff started to cry.

"What's the matter, baby?" Jim wanted to know.

"Nothing. I'm just so fucking happy, is all." They ate in relative silence, occasionally smiling at each other. Then, when they were finished and the apartment was cleaned up, they sat down in the living room. They sat in separate chairs facing each other. Looking at Jim, Jeff asked. "Do you want to talk first or shall I?"

"I brought up the subject and I'll start." Jim got quiet for a while, collecting his thoughts and finally began. "Most of what I'm going to tell you, I had forgotten about. It certainly had no meaning to me until I began to think of why I never had a clue that I might be gay. So here goes.

"My brother Tom is five years older than I, about your age. My folks both worked, so during the hours between 2 PM and 6 PM we were pretty much alone at home. Two or three afternoons a week, Tom's friend, Mike, came over and the two boys went up to Tom's room and closed the door. One day I came home from school and headed for my room. I had to pass Tom's room on the way and saw that the door was partially open. I clearly heard moaning and groaning and peeked in cautiously. Tom and Mike were sitting side by side on Tom's bed and mutually masturbating each other. I was old enough to know what they were doing but hadn't yet tried it myself. Suddenly Tom screamed, "I'm cuuuumiiiing!" I saw this white stuff squirt from his cock on to his pubic hair, up to his stomach and his chest. Mike followed Tom and shot his load a few seconds later. I was fascinated by what I had seen, but feared being caught, so I silently crept to my room and stayed there until I heard them go downstairs.

"For the next several days I tried doing what they had done, but I couldn't get hard and nothing really happened. Then one day I fantasized that Mike was doing it to me and I began to swell and harden as much as an eleven year old can. I felt the orgasm building in my groin. It was my first time and it was heavenly. My cum was thin and translucent, not like Tom's, and I worried about that. Jeff, my love, today for the first time, I realize that all my masturbation fantasies are about men, usually Mike."

Jeff wanted to say something, but sensed that Jim was not finished so he remained silent. He was right, and Jim continued.

"In college my room mate was a life long friend, Jerry Rubin. I never thought about it until now, but while there were girls coming and going in all the other dorm rooms, neither of us seemed sexually active. As for me, it was because Francie and I already had an understanding, and I just didn't think about whether Jerry screwed around or not.

"One night, I heard Jerry making strange noises from his bed. I quietly got up and went to investigate. As my eyes got used to the dark I could see that he was jacking off. Not being one to interrupt so intimate an act, I crept stealthily back in bed and started to jack off too. Jeff, you know by now, I'm a screamer, and when I came, I let loose. Jerry realized what I was doing, and he started to laugh. Then I started to laugh too, and we both agreed to do 'it' whenever we felt the need without worrying about what the other guy thought. We jerked off as much as we wanted from then on. We did it when the other was present, but we never did it mutually like Tom and Mike. I must admit, I thought about asking Jerry how he would feel about doing it to each other, but I remained silent."

"I don't see how..." Jeff began, but Jim interrupted.

"I'm not quite through. On the evening before graduation day, which was to be our last day in the dorm, Jerry and I joined a bunch of other guys at a local pub. We really tore one on. Honey, I was so drunk I don't remember leaving the bar or going to the dorm. When I woke the next morning, Jerry and I were in his bed in our birthday suits, wrapped up in each other's arms. I unraveled myself and found dried, crusty cum all over both of us. I have no idea if we just did our usual hand waving or something more happened. Whatever had occurred, I had no guilt feelings. The only emotion I had was anger that I couldn't remember anything about the night before. Here's the kicker. Jerry came out to me before we left the room for the last time. He begged me not to judge him because he was gay, and to please still be his friend. He told me how hard it was to keep his hands off me all these years, and how often he wanted to do the masturbating for me. I was dumbfounded, but didn't have the nerve to tell him that it would have been fine with me if he had, and that I had experienced the same thoughts about mutual masturbation.

"Now, don't you think I should have suspected myself of being gay from these incidents?"

Jeff hesitated, and before he could answer, the phone rang sharply. Jim looked at the caller ID. "It's Francie," he said, "I'd better answer it."

"Hi honey," he said, and then he grew silent. As Francie began to talk, Jim motioned Jeff to put his ear near the phone so he could hear too. This is what Francie said.

"Jim, just listen and don't interrupt me. What I am going to say is going to hurt you. I need to say it fast and then hang up on you. I don't want you to answer me back. Jim, honey, I met an Aussie out here who's rich as Croesus. He wants to marry me and take me back to Australia. Jim, when he made love to me the first time, there were real fireworks, and I knew that there really was never anything between you and me. We've been friends since kindergarten. For God sakes we're more like brother and sister, and I hope it can remain like that.

"I'm going to fax you my power of attorney for sale of the apartment and my car. Please sell the apartment furnished and tell Ron that I don't care what he lists it for, or how much he has to adjust his commission, as long as I clear $200,000. Just please do it for me. As for the car, you'll need wheels now, so sell it to yourself for $1.00. That will be my farewell gift to you. I'll contact you from Sydney and I really do love you as a brother. Please visit us first chance you get." Before Jim could answer, she hung up.

Jim looked at Jeff to answer his question before he asked it. "Ron Richardson is a mutual friend and a realtor," he explained. Then he added, "Can you believe this shit? Wow this is quite a surprise. Well that's one hurdle less for us, and since you're getting a divorce, I guess we're legal." He grabbed Jeff and they started to kiss him wildly. Jeff started to push Jim toward the bedroom, but Jim pulled away and said there would be no sex until he heard Jeff's story.

"Mine is quick," Jeff said. "I was about 15 when this happened. It was about 10 AM one morning and I got a bad case of the runs in Math class, so I grabbed my stuff and went home. Both my folks worked so I didn't expect to find anyone at home. In addition to the garage overhead door, there was a regular door on the side of the house leading in to the garage. That's the one I always used. As soon as I entered the garage through the side door, I got a shock. There was a car parked in the garage that I recognized immediately. It belonged to my parents' best friends, my godparents, Brian and Colleen O'Toole. To say that I was surprised would be an understatement. We lived in a one story ranch so I didn't have to worry about creaky stairs when I went to investigate what was going on. The house was really quiet, but as I crept toward my parents' bedroom, I heard soft moans. The door was wide open. Standing where I couldn't be seen, I peeked in. Brian and my dad were naked in bed doing a great game of 69 on each other. Before I could recover from the shock, they disengaged from each other. My dad reached into his night stand and took out some lube. He lubed Brian's ass and then his cock, which was magnificent by the way. Brian lay on his back and placed his legs on my dad's shoulders. Then my dad entered Brian so effortlessly you knew it was something they were used to doing.

"Here's the thing. If I was straight, I would have screamed and yelled and bopped them both in the eye. Instead I was so horny I nearly split my pants. Worse yet, I had incestuous feeling for my hunky dad. Needless to say, I got out of the house as quietly as I could. For all I know Brian and dad are still going at it. I don't want to know. After that, my masturbation fantasies revolved around that scene. Every time I jerk off, I picture my dad fucking Brian. Looking back now, my reaction to my dad's fucking another man, should have clued me in to the possibility that I was gay. What do you think?"

"I think," Jim said "that we should give up the analysis and climb into bed. All these stories have made me pretty horny. We still have lots to talk about and lots to plan, but like you say, 'tomorrow is another day.' "

"Now it's my turn to delay. I want to run something by you." Jeff said very seriously. "We are both going to need a place to move to, because in a way we are both being forced to vacate. What would you say to us buying this place? We can offer Francie $200,000 clear without any additional costs to her. We'll pay any incidental closing costs. This place is worth at least $50,000 more than she wants, so everyone wins, and I get to start the rest of my life loving you, and being your partner forever. Please, please say yes, and I'll start moving in this weekend."

"Wow! That's an overwhelming thought." Jim responded. "I'd say yes if I could afford to pay half, but I don't want to share something with you unless it's 50/50, and God knows I can't afford to pay for what you are proposing."

"OK. I understand." Jeff said. "How about this? I come up with the down payment and we mortgage the rest. We'll pay the mortgage and all household expenses, maintenance fees, etc., 50/50. You can give me a note for half the down payment. We'll arrange an easy pay plan." Then with a smile, Jeff added, "I assure you, you'll be able to afford it."

"Man that is so fantastic. OK. You win. God, this is so exciting. I'll call Francie on her cell tomorrow morning. I need to know how to reach her, her husband's name and address, a million things. Now can we please get each other laid?"

CHAPTER 4

"Now can I please get laid?" Jim grabbed Jeff's hand and headed towards the bedroom, but once again the phone rang. "I think celibacy is the order of the night." Jim sounded despondent as he went to answer the phone.

He looked at the caller ID and picked up the phone. "Hi Mom," he said as cheerily as possible. He listened for a moment and then said, "No, Francie isn't back yet, but I'd be glad to come to dinner Friday evening, if I can bring a guest." Some time passed as he listened to his mother and then he replied, "Well Mom. It's my boss. You didn't give me a chance to tell you, but I got a great job with great pay, in an up and coming company, and my boss is a super guy. I started yesterday." There was some more small talk as his mom quizzed him. He avoided her question as to how much his salary was, and he finally hung up.

"Whew," he said as he wiped his brow in a mock fashion. "We're having dinner at my folk's Friday evening and no excuses. We need to get all our hurdles over with as quickly as possible. We're coming out to them on Friday, and then it's your turn with your folks. After that it will be easy. I have one sibling and you have none. Our friends will have to like it or lump it. I'll understand if you want to stay in the closet with your clients."

Jeff said that he thought that would be on a case to case basis, and Jim looked at him imploringly and said. "Can I get laid now?"

Jim sent Jeff ahead into the bedroom while he shut the lights and put *their* apartment to bed. When he got to the bedroom, Jeff was fully undressed and warming the water in the shower. Man that guy is fast, Jim thought. In record time Jim undressed and headed for the shower just as Jeff entered it. The shower was smaller than Jeff's so they could not avoid intimacy. They embraced, hugged and kissed. They each washed the other's front and back, paying special attention to their throbbing cocks in the front and their love holes in the back. Reluctantly, they left the shower and towel dried their bodies, each helping the other, stealing kisses all the while.

Jim took Jeff's hand and led him to the bed, which he hadn't bothered to make up when he went on his interview yesterday. (Was it only yesterday?) "Jim," Jeff asked, "will you do me a favor? Will you pretend to be Brian and I'll pretend to be my father. It'll be like my fantasy come true."

"Sure thing and then next time we'll mutually masturbate each other and I'll pretend you're Mike. That way we can put our old fantasies away and make new ones that belong just to us." Jim put a palm on each of Jeff's cheeks and kissed him. Then he went to his night stand and found the condoms and lube which he handed to Jeff. Jeff looked at the condoms and shrugged his shoulder.

"I know what you're thinking." Jim said. We haven't been with other men. But I don't want to go bareback. Since Francie's call I'm not sure who she has been with and I want us to play it safe. Let's get tested really soon, OK?" Jeff nodded in agreement.

Jim lay on his back and Jeff lubed Jim's ass hole really well. He asked Jim to roll the condom on his beautiful cock and then he lubed it. He positioned it right at Jim's entrance. Jim grabbed Jeff's shaft and held it steady as Jeff slowly entered him. It hurt a little until Jeff passed the sphincter. Then it slid in quickly. Jeff held still while both men enjoyed the moment and then he began to go in and out slowly. At some point Jeff's cock began to make contact with Jim's prostate and Jim began to moan in pure ecstasy.

"Stop!" Jim yelled at Jeff. "I'm coming and I want to delay it." Jeff stopped and lowered himself on Jim's body. Their lips met, and their tongues caressed each other. After a while, Jim began to move his hips informing Jeff to get going again. As soon as Jeff started pumping again, it was over for Jim. With one loud scream he squirted one stream after another up his belly and chest. As he did, he involuntarily contracted his ass hole and that put Jeff over the edge also. Jim could feel him pulsating inside of him. Eventually Jeff fell over Jim spreading Jim's cum all over both of them. They lay that way until Jeff's cock got so limp that it slid right out.

Jeff got out of bed and flushed the full condom down the toilet. He took one of the towels they had used to dry themselves, and he cleaned the rest of his body and did the same to Jim. Neither felt like showering again and decided that they would wait until morning.

They lay wrapped in each other's arms. If they could they would have melted into each other and become two souls in one body. Then Jeff, ever the practical one, said, "Honey, I usually run every morning and I brought shorts and my running shoes in the bag. After that I'll need to shower, dress, and maybe make some coffee and something to go with it. We need about 25 minutes to drive down town. For now we'll park my car at my apartment and walk to the office. I figure that to get to the office by 9, we have to set the alarm for 6:30. Is that OK with you?" he asked.

"Well, love, here's another coincidence. I run about 2 miles every morning also, so 6:30 would be fine except for one thing. We have to shower separately, or we'll never get out of the house, so let's make it 6:15.

"It's a deal." Jeff answered, and Jim set his alarm clock. It just took a few moments after that, and they fell asleep in each other's arms, their limp cocks mashed together.

At about 2 AM, Jim was awakened by a ringing telephone. It took him a moment to realize it was the fax machine. He tried to get out of bed without disturbing Jeff. By the time he got to the office, several pages had been printed out. He read the cover sheet and it was the powers of attorney from Francie. There was also a short note in which she gave him vital information. They were leaving on Sunday; her future husband was John Smith (She had to be kidding.) His address in Sydney was 128B Abernathy Street. She would let him know the postal code, if any, at a later date and he could reach her on her cell phone until Sunday. After that he could reach them at John's telephone number which was the same as his fax number. She gave him the number in Australia. Then as a PS, she added a request to please give all her clothing to charity. (Francie was really severing all ties with home, and Jim wondered if she wasn't being too hasty.) She wrote that she had her jewelry with her and John wanted her to get a whole new wardrobe, appropriate for the Australian climate.

Jim figured that she was still awake, so he dialed her on her cell. Francie picked up the phone immediately. He wished her well and said that he would always be a brother to her and that she was right to see that their relationship didn't stand a chance. He told her he had gotten his dream job, but he said nothing about his relationship with Jeff. Finally he told her that he had a buyer for the apartment and didn't have to go through a real estate agent. She was delighted and couldn't thank him enough. He hung up the phone and turned to see Jeff leaning against the door frame totally naked with a solid hard on.

"Want to do the Mike thing?" he asked.

"Sure." Jim answered.

When they were done, and their fantasies had become reality, they were ready to make new fantasies and they fell asleep once again, hugging each other tightly.

The morning routine went exactly as they had planned. Before they shut the apartment to leave for work, Jeff advised Jim to take his powers with him. In the car Jeff told him that his old college room mate was a tax attorney. They often referred clients to each other, and Jeff often sought his advice on sticky tax matters. He said he'd call his friend to find out when they could see him about drawing up a contract for the sale of the house. He was sure that the work would be done pro bono or for a nominal fee. Suddenly Jeff began to laugh.

"What's up, lover?" Jim asked

"I just thought of something funny. My friend is gay, and often when we are working together late, we'll go for a drink afterwards. He always asks me if we should go to his place or mine, meaning a gay bar or a straight bar. Of course, I always laugh and say that we should go to my place. Next time I'll say, to his place, and see his reaction. Wait until he realizes that in all those college years, we never had sex together. He kept trying to 'convert' me and I always laughed at him. He'll kill me."

They got to the office together, and Jeanine gave them both a warm and knowing smile. "So when are you two moving in together?" she asked.

"Sooner than you think." Jeff replied.

They both went to their offices and Jim picked up where he had left off the afternoon before. At about 10 AM Jeff came into Jim's office. He could have buzzed, but he wanted to lay his eyes on Jim. He just couldn't get enough of him. "Our attorney is going to see us at 4 PM. We don't have to leave but five minutes earlier. He's just across the street." And just like that, Jeff returned to his office. Jim picked up on the phrase, "our attorney," and he smiled to himself.

An hour later, Jeff appeared at Jim's door again. "Saturday evening at my folks. It will be my turn to come out." And as quick as that, he was gone.

It was Jeff's turn to pay for lunch this day. They had begun to really enjoy their lunch hour together. They could relax, enjoy each other's company and play footsies under the table. They could even fondle each other occasionally. But when they were in the office, it was strictly business.

As usual Jim was so wrapped up in his work, he lost track of time. Suddenly there stood Jeff, telling him to get his papers together. It was time to see the lawyer. They crossed the street and entered the office building directly across from theirs. The elevator took them to the third floor where they entered a nicely furnished, but unpretentious office. The receptionist told them that Mr. Costello would be right out.

They sat in the reception area talking quietly and allowing their knees to touch whenever possible, until they heard a deep voice say, "Jeff, where the fuck have you been? You haven't called me for lunch for nearly a week now." Jim and Jeff jumped to their feet.

"Michael, let me introduce you to my new associate, Jim Lester." Jim and Michael extended their hands for a business like hand shake, and finally got a good look at each other.

"Mike!" Jim yelled.

"Jim!" Michael yelled back, and they fell into a not so business like bear hug, while Jeff stared in disbelief.

"Jeff" Jim explained. This is my brother Tom's friend, Mike."

"*The* Mike?" Jeff asked with a knowing smile. "God, it's a small world."

"What's all this private joke stuff?" Michael wanted to know.

"I can't tell you now, but I swear I will before the day is out." Jim promised.

"How's Tom?" Michael asked.

"He married Melissa Remington. You must remember her. They started dating in their junior year in high school, about the time you stopped coming around." Jim added that as part of his private joke. "They have a 3 year old son and a daughter on the way."

"Man," Michael sighed. "This is amazing. Well, let's get going." He headed for his office and Jim and Jeff followed.

Jim showed Michael his powers of attorney for the house and the car. He told Michael what terms had been agreed upon between the buyer and seller. Then he set off the bomb. He informed Michael that the buyers were Jeff and himself. They were going to secure a mortgage in both their names for $150,000 and Jeff would put down $50,000. Michael was to prepare a promissory note between them for a debt of $25,000 to be paid whenever and without interest. "That's it in a nutshell." Jim concluded.

Michael was silent for a while and then he shouted, "You fuckers. That's it in a nutshell? What the fuck is going on here?" Michael had a way with words.

"Well Michael, let's put it this way," Jeff said. Tonight we'll go for drinks to your place." Michael got hysterical. He laughed so hard he started to cough and Jeff got up to slap him on the back.

"You are a fucker, Jeff." He said after he collected himself. "I've been trying to convert you for years and now you spring this on me. And you," he said turning to Jim, "what were all those giggly glances about when Jeff asked if I was *the* Mike?"

"Oh what the fuck," Jim answered. "It can't matter now. You see, Mike, I once caught you and Tom jacking each other off. I realize that's not significant, but as I told Jeff, from that time on my masturbation fantasy was that you were jerking me off, and that is what is significant."

Fucking unbelievable. This gets more and more incredible. I could have had you all these years." Michael was still laughing. "Let's go get those drinks, and I want to hear everything."

Since Jeff and Jim had walked to work from Jeff's place, Michael got his car from the public garage next door to his building. He drove a few miles to the section of town Jeff and Jim were aware of, but had never been to. It was commonly known as "Gaytown." It was early for any crowds and Michael was able to pull up right in front of a bar called, "Chuck's Place." When they entered the bar, the newbies were surprised. Both had expected to find a disco, a DJ playing loud music, and half naked hunks gyrating to the beat, something like Babylon in "Queer as Folk." This was a very conservative cocktail lounge like any straight lounge they had ever been to.

They found a table in a quiet corner. Michael told them that there was no table service. He asked what they would like to drink, and went to the bar to take care of the first round. When he returned, he toasted his two friends, and said rather sternly, "Talk!"

Jeff filled him in on everything to date, how they met, fell in love, made love, his pending divorce, Jim's broken engagement, how each had fulfilled the other's masturbation fantasies, how those fantasies had begun in the first place, the upcoming "coming out party" at Jim's parents this Friday evening, and on and on and on. Michael was amazed and beamed with happiness. In fact, he had a tear in his eye. "God, I am so happy for you two, and delighted to have you as friends." He then proceeded to give them a little gay orientation. He told them where the GLCC was and that they could get tested on Tuesday evenings, and pick up results on Friday evening. He recommended the best gay restaurants and bars, and informed them which straight businesses were gay friendly and which to avoid.

They were on their third round of drinks, but now they were drinking cokes, when Jim heard a familiar voice yelling and running toward him. Jim looked toward the voice, threw his head on the table, and exclaimed, "I can't take any more surprises." There stood Jerry Rubin, recent and former college room mate, and masturbation mate without compare. He and Jerry embraced, and unexpectedly, Jerry kissed Jim chastely on the lips.

Jim introduced Jerry to Jeff and Michael. When Jerry shook Michael's hand, a look passed between them and Jim and Jeff could feel electricity in the room. Jim thought, I know that feeling. I know that look. Jerry sat down with them, and looked at Jim.

"What are you doing here?" Jerry asked suspiciously. So Jeff and Jim repeated an abbreviated version of what they had told Michael. "Wow! To think I wasted four years when I could have had you." Jerry joked. It seemed that everyone regretted not coming on to Jim or Jeff.

They made small talk for a while. Michael and Jerry couldn't stop staring at each other and smiling. Once or twice their hands dropped below the table and Jim had a suspicion that something was going on. Michael informed Jeff and Jim that after 9 PM there was a piano player here and they could dance together if they wanted to. Jeff said, "Not tonight, ambulance chaser. How about driving us home or should we grab a cab?"

"No, I'll take you home." He turned to Jerry and asked, "Why don't you come with us? Then you and I can get better acquainted while these two wusses have their hot tea and toast, and go off to bed with their socks on." Everyone laughed.

After Michael dropped them off and before he drove off, Jim was certain he saw Michael reach across the console of his car and put his hand high up on Jerry's thigh.

What a hoot! Jim thought.

CHAPTER 5

Friday afternoon, at about 4 PM, Jeanine buzzed Jim. "Michael Costello is on the line." she informed him.

"Greetings pal." Jim opened the conversation.

"Greetings faggot." Was his glib response. Jim knew he was pulling his leg and laughed along with Mike. (He just couldn't get himself to call his old friend, Michael, like everyone else did.) Mike continued, "I've got all the necessary documents to fax to Francie. If you can come over right away and sign everything, I can fax it out tonight so everything will be there for her when she gets to Sydney. And, sweetheart, I took the liberty of preparing domestic partnership agreements, living trusts, health surrogate papers and a few other things you guys should have. I'll explain it all when I see you."

"Let me put you on hold for a sec while I check with Jeff." Jim hit the hold button and buzzed Jeff. They rarely did that. Usually they walked over to the other's office so they could catch yet another glimpse of perfection. Boy, were they in love. Jim explained what Mike had called about and Jeff said that would be fine. He told Jim to wrap it up for the day, the weekend, actually.

Ten minutes later, they were signing document after document, including the new registration for Jim's car. Michael had taken care of everything and finally he announced that they were free to go. He also knew that they would be coming out to Jim's parents very shortly and he wished them luck. He gave each one a big hug, and as they left he said, mostly to Jim, "I want to know how Tom takes the news, and by the way faggot, Jerry and I have a hot date tonight."

"Well have fun you two and do everything I would do." Jim leered at Mike.

In the elevator Jim said to Jeff, "Wouldn't it be fantastic (he wanted to say fabulous, but resisted the urge) if those two became an item?"

Two hours later, freshly showered and dressed, Jim pulled Jeff's car into his parents' driveway. "Oh shit," he blurted out to no one in particular.

"What's wrong?" Jeff wanted to know.

"That car in the driveway is Tom's. He and his family must be here too."

"That's a good thing." Jeff consoled Jim. "Don't we want to spread the news as quickly as possible?"

"I guess so."

Jim knocked on the front door, but entered without anyone inside answering. Tom greeted Jim with a bone crushing bear hug. When he released him, he smiled broadly and joked. "It's about time you made some money and stopped being such a burden to your family." He looked at Jeff and extended his hand. At the same time he said, "You must be Jeff, his financial benefactor."

Jim then introduced Jeff to Melissa, young Tommie, Jr. and his parents. When he introduced Jeff to his parents, he purposely introduced them as Mom and Dad and did not use their given names, John and Sharon. Nobody noticed except Jeff.

John ushered everyone into the living room for cocktails before dinner. Jim had decided he would tell everyone about his relationship with Jeff when they were having dessert. No use spoiling the dinner, if things went badly. So over cocktails he told about Francie's phone call. Everyone was upset, but Jim assured them he was fine with it and it was for the best, and he was getting a car out of the deal. He refrained from mentioning the apartment just yet. Then proudly he told about seeing Jeff's ad in the newspaper, getting an interview, and how great the two of them worked together and got along so well. He thought about it for the moment, and finally added the news of Jeff's pending divorce. More regrets were expressed and Jeff assured everyone, as Jim had, that it was for the best.

Looking directly at Tom, Jim decided to drop the first small bomb. "Tom, you'll never guess who Jeff's lawyer is." Without giving Tom a chance to guess, he added, "Mike Costello, your old high school buddy. But everyone calls him Michael now."

There was no question that Tom cringed a little, but he said nothing. "He sends his regards to you. He said he'd love to hear from you," Jim looked for more reaction. None.

Finally Tom said, "Tell him I send my regards too. Now, mom, isn't dinner ready yet?"

"Yes," she said and asked everyone to please come into the dining room. Melissa and Tom sat on one side and Jim and Jeff on the other side of the table. John and Sharon sat at the head and foot. Little Tommie had been fed earlier and was in the den watching television. Dinner was delicious. Sharon served salad, hot dinner rolls, roast chicken with mashed potatoes and grilled vegetables. For dessert she made a mouth watering strawberry shortcake, served with coffee or tea.

The big moment had arrived. Nervously, Jim stood up. "Listen up everyone. There's something I need to tell you, make that, must tell you." For some reason he looked directly into his father's eyes. John misread his son's intent and panicked.

"What's wrong?" his voice pleaded with his son.

"Nothing's wrong Dad. In fact, for the first time in my life everything is just perfect. I am the happiest I have ever been in my entire life." Now he looked directly into Jeff's eyes. Jeff smiled encouragement to his partner. "Folks," he began, "Jeff and I are buying Francie's apartment together. Don't get the wrong idea. We are not going to be room mates. We have committed to each other and we are going to be partners in life." He stopped talking. The silence was dreadful and he grabbed Jeff's hand for strength.

Tom was the first to speak. "Are you saying that you and Jeff are gay? You must be kidding. It can't be. Neither of you fits..." he hesitated.

"the stereotype." Jim finished the sentence for him. More deafening silence. Then John stood up and approached his son. He grabbed Jim's arm and pulled him toward him and embraced him tenderly.

"Son," he said. I love you. I love you unconditionally. I'm particularly glad to hear that you have never been happier in your life and it's your life to enjoy. Thank you for your honesty and courage. I know how hard this must have been for you." He kissed Jim on the cheek and turned to Jeff. Welcome to the family," he said. Jeff jumped up and John embraced him.

Then Sharon ran to her son and smothered him with kisses. "Did you ever think that this would make a difference in how any of us felt about you?

Nonsense, if you did." Then she embraced Jeff, kissed him in a very motherly fashion and said, "Yes Jeff, welcome to the family."

Tom had remained silent, unable to move until Melissa whispered in his ear, "He's your baby brother darling. Show him you love him no matter what."

That started Tom crying, and then Jim started to cry uncontrollably. The two brothers embraced, sobbing like babies. Jim's head was on his taller brother's shoulders, and Tom whispered into Jim's ear, "You got yourself one hell of a good looking guy." Jim's sobs turned to laughter as Tom disengaged him and went over to Jeff. "Listen Bro," he said. You hurt my kid brother and you answer to me. Hear?"

"Loud and clear," Jeff answered as Melissa came over to Jeff and kissed him on the cheek. Just then Tommie came into the room and Melissa asked him to come and meet his new uncle, Jeff.

"If you're my uncle, are you going to buy me presents too?" he asked and everyone began to laugh and cry at the same time.

Then Tom asked, "Does this mean I have to change accountants and use you two guys?"

"Absolutely," Jim and Jeff said simultaneously. Then Jim added, "You might think of switching lawyers too. Mike really wants to see you and to be your friend. Really Tom, he's no threat to you." Somehow Tom knew what Jim meant, and it was OK.

"I promise. I'll call him."

The lovers drove home in contented silence. How happy they were. Jim's parents did not lose a son, they indeed gained another one. Jeff already felt that he was an accepted part of Jim's family. He couldn't help wonder how things would go with his family. Of course, Jim sensed what Jeff was thinking. He turned to his partner, who was driving, and said, "Don't worry, hon, it will be fine."

But I'm afraid that my father will act as if I'm going to hell in order to cover his own indiscretions. Well, I'll worry about it tomorrow. After all, tomorrow is another day." They both started to laugh.

That night they slept at Jeff's place. Their love making was unhurried, slow, sensual, reciprocal, and mostly oral. Their passions were designed to give each other maximum pleasure. They knew that from now on they had all the time in the world and so they rushed nothing. They sucked each other's cocks alternately until they would feel an orgasm coming. Then each would stop and they would switch positions. They switched several times until they could stop no longer and first Jeff came with his usual guttural moans and then

Jim came with his loud scream of joy. They swallowed each other's juices not missing a drop. The sheets were perfectly clean.

The next morning was Saturday, Jeff's moving day. They got up early and went to pick up the UHaul they had arranged to rent. They also bought packing boxes and packing tape. They spent the morning packing Jeff's stuff and loading it into the truck. Once Jeff's clothes and toiletries were packed, there was little left. Jeff realized how few material possessions he had gathered during his marriage. Everything in the apartment belonged to Marie, and he vowed that things would change in his new life with Jim.

By 4 PM that afternoon, everything they had taken from Jeff's apartment was in their soon to be new home. Michael was waiting to hear where to wire the down payment and Jeff had contacted his banker regarding a mortgage. Still it felt like it was their place already. After they returned the truck, the first thing they did was to remove Jeff's clothing from the packing boxes and replace it with Francie's stuff. Jeff had heard of a Thrift Shop that donated its profits to AIDS charities and he said he would call them on Monday morning to pick the boxes up. Then they hung Jeff's clothing in the closet and put his socks, underwear, shirts, etc. in the vacated dresser drawers. By six they were done. They showered quickly, and started out to Jeff's parents. Jim drove his new car.

Jeff introduced Jim to his parents as his new associate, and introduced his folks as Tucker and Maryann Simmons. There was only to be the four of them to dinner. Jeff had half expected to see the O'Tooles and even remarked about it. His father said that he had sounded so serious when he made the date, that he thought it best to omit them this time. Jeff could hardly remember when the O'Tooles were not at one of his parent's dinner parties. They were his godparents, after all, and their daughter, MacKenzie was like a sister to him.

Like Jim, Jeff waited until dessert to drop the bomb. He stood up and began, "Mom, Dad, you know that Marie has asked for a divorce. I'm not contesting it and I'll be single in less than a month. I met Jim when he came for an interview and it was love at first sight for both of us. We've committed to each other, and we are life partners. We've bought a condo together, and I moved in this afternoon." Then, taking a hint from Jim's scrapbook, he added, "I have never been happier in my life."

Jim looked at his dad. Tucker was fuming and turning red. "Get out of my house, you faggot and take this thing with you." Jeff didn't move. He knew that his father was crying out at his own inability to have a life with Brian O'Toole. Wisely, he waited. This was exactly what he expected to happen and he had prepared himself. Then Tucker started crying and collapsed in his chair. "I'm sorry son," he said. You know I didn't mean it."

Maryann went to her son and embraced him. "We both love you very much, my darling. Your dad didn't mean what he said. Please forgive him."

Then she turned to Jim and said, "I am sure we'll learn to love you too. If you make Jeff happier than he has ever been before, you must be a wonderful person." She placed a small peck of a kiss on Jim's cheek.

In the meantime Jeff kept staring at his father. He realized the anguish he was in by keeping his own dark secret all these years. His father was sobbing uncontrollably so Jeff took his arm and said, "Let's go into the den. I need to talk to you alone." They went into the den leaving Jim and Maryann to get better acquainted.

Jeff decided to be blunt and honest with his father. He came right to the point. "Dad I know that your tears are not for me. I know that you are overjoyed for me and Jim. Your tears are for you and Brian."

"Hh…how did you know?" Tucker stuttered.

"I got sick at school one day and came home early. I saw you making love with Brian. I thought I should be angry with you, but instead I felt compassion. I wondered at the anguish you must be feeling, so obviously in love with Brian and still in love with Mom. If I had the courage I would have gone into the room and consoled both of you, but I ran out of the house. I still feel that compassion, dad, and I love you deeply and strongly. If there is anything that either Jim or I can do to ease the burden, please let us know." Jeff omitted telling his father how aroused he had gotten and how horny he had become for his dad.

Tucker began to sob uncontrollably. He and his son hugged each other, and Jeff ran his hand up and down Tucker's back to console him. Finally Tucker said, "I met Brian on my first day at work. It was his first day also. They sent us away for a week's orientation in St. Louis, where we shared a hotel room. Even though we were both newlyweds, we fell in love, and neither of us could explain it. I have been in anguish all my life and sometime soon, I'd like to sit down and talk to you about it. Maybe if I do, I can unburden some of my pain. I'm glad that unlike me, you are admitting who you are. At this point I wouldn't do anything to hurt your mother, but it's a great comfort to me to know that my son is living the life he was meant to have. It's also great to know that I have an ally in you. Can I tell Brian that you know about us?"

"Of course you can. I imagine it will comfort him too."

"By the way," Tucker added as a final thought, "Jim seems like one hell of a nice guy."

"He is Dad, and I have no words to describe how much I love him."

Father and son went back to the dining room with their arms around their shoulders. They found Jim and Maryann holding hands and deep in conversation. She was saying to Jim, "Please call us mom and dad, Jim."

"That will be a pleasure." He answered.

After that Jeff told his folks about Jim's 'interview,' the sparks that flew between them and the love that was immediately evident. His parent's smiled with obvious pleasure and acceptance. When it was time to leave, Jeff gave them his new address and telephone number. The four of them hugged each other and the boys left for home.

When they entered into the hallway and locked the entrance door, they immediately fell into each other's arms, kissing, hugging, fondling their bulging packages, and moaning softly to one another how much each loved the other. All the while, bits and pieces of their clothing were being removed, leaving a trail from the hallway to the bedroom.

Next, still wrapped up together they started the shower and when the water temperature satisfied both of them, they got in. They soaped each other, massaged each other, stroked their bulging, hungry cocks, sucked each other, and rubbed their cocks in the cracks of each other's love holes until they were both in frenzy. Finally they came out of the shower, cleaner and hornier than either could ever remember. They tumbled into bed where they kissed with hungry tongues, cocks rubbing sensuously together.

"Fuck me!" each yelled to the other. Even though they had not yet been tested, Jim reached into the dresser drawer and removed the lube. Condoms were not an option tonight.

"Me first." Jim shouted. His lust was uncontrollable. He put a generous amount of lube on Jeff's cock and then lubed his ass hole. He lay down on his back and as Jeff got into position he put his legs on Jeff's shoulders, and yelled, "Now love, now!" Jeff entered him like a ramrod and Jim screamed in pain and pleasure. Jeff waited, and then began stroking gently. Now Jim's pain turned to pure pleasure and he shouted. "Harder, harder." Jeff increased the length and speed of his stroking. Jim's moans suddenly turned to a scream of pure joy as he came, spewing his juices up his belly and chest. Jeff came seconds later. and collapsed on Jim. For the first time, Jim could feel Jeff's love juices fill his insides, and he began to sob, great gasping sobs of pure joy and happiness.

They lay stuck together by Jim's cum, kissing slowly and sensually. The lust had ebbed and the love they felt for each other had been magnified to new heights. Their families knew and approved of their union. The hurdles were gone. Life was about to begin for them and it was good.

Jeff whispered to Jim. "Do you think you are ready to fuck me yet?"

CHAPTER SIX

On the night that Jeff came out to his parents and introduced them to Jim, Tucker was unable to sleep. He crept out of bed as quietly as possible, and went to his den. There he pulled out several old picture albums and reviewed Jeff's life through the fading photographs. He began to sob silently, tears falling down his cheeks. He observed that Jeff had been absolutely correct in his analysis. He wasn't crying because he had a gay son. He was crying for the loss of the life he and Brian might have had. If only they had met before they were married instead of after the fact. How different things might have been. But then, there would be no Jeff and no Mackenzie. That thought was even more unbearable.

His mind boggled at the thought that Jeff had known about him and Brian for about twelve years now, and had kept their secret. He knew it was partially to protect Maryann and Colleen, but Jeff had made it quite clear that it was out of compassion for Brian and him as well. He couldn't love his son more at this moment than he had all of Jeff's life. He tried to imagine how traumatic it must have been for Jeff when he caught them in the act. It would have shocked him even more to know that the scene had actually turned Jeff on.

He put the albums away and sat down in his reclining chair. His thoughts turned to Jim. He was an absolute hunk. Jeff had good taste and was a lucky son of a gun. But then, Jeff was a hunk also.

Tuck smiled to himself as his body began to drift away into an uneasy sleep. Unbidden and unwanted thoughts began to invade his mind. He began to envision Jeff and Jim naked in bed together. *They were wrapped up in one another's arms, kissing with open mouths and thrusting tongues. Then they twisted their bodies around into a 69 position and took each other tenderly, passionately, sensuously into each other's mouths.* Tuck was suddenly aware that he was getting turned on by thoughts of his own son and his son's lover. He tried desperately to change his fantasy from Jeff and Jim to Brian and him, but it wasn't working. He wasn't even aware that he had pulled down his boxers and was gently stroking his cock. His fantasy suddenly changed. It was like a badly edited movie. There was no segueing. It just went from one scene to another. *Now Jim was flat on his back and Jeff was riding him like a bucking bronco. Jim's cock was high up Jeff's ass and they were fucking hard.*

Then again without segueing, Jim was gone and it was Tucker who Jeff was riding. The eroticism of that scene was just too much for Tuck. Suddenly he came in a spasmodic orgasm. He tried to stifle his scream but was only partially successful. Fortunately Maryann was a deep sleeper.

He went into the powder room off the front hall and cleaned himself as best he could. Then he went back to bed, but he couldn't sleep.

When Jeff and Jim got home that night, they were euphoric. They had come out to their families and there were no dire consequences. Even Jim's macho brother, Tom, was OK with it. Tom's son was thrilled to have another uncle to give him gifts. The two young men found it necessary to celebrate their union. It was a tough job but they had to do it.

During their love making, when Jeff was about to enter Jim, he suddenly started fantasizing that he was entering his father. That was a masturbation fantasy he hadn't had since he met Jim. He tried to change the fantasy but it was just too hot and he came very prematurely.

"That was fast," Jim observed. "Let's do it again." He was laughing as he said it.

"Give me thirty seconds to recuperate," Jeff parried back. It actually took about thirty minutes.

It was mid morning the next day, Sunday, when Jeff got a call from his dad. "I'm calling for Brian," he said. "He doesn't have your new number and he wants to invite you over for a barbeque this afternoon. Mackenzie, Peter and the baby will be here, and I think you should come. I haven't said anything to them yet, and you might want to do the honors, especially to Mackenzie. None of them even knows about Jim's existence."

"Of course we'll come, Dad. They are family, after all, and we should be honest and come out to the rest of the family." Jeff had forgotten about his 'sister.' Last night they thought the coming out parties was all over, and here we go again, he thought.

Immediately after he hung up, the phone rang again. Jeff picked it up and heard Michael ask without a hello, "So how'd it go?"

"It went great. We're now officially out to everyone except my 'sister' and that's on the agenda for this afternoon. So far everyone's fine with it."

Michael still harbored the feeling that Brian and Tucker had something going on. He felt it from the first evening they had met in his college dorm room when he and Jeff became room mates. The more he knew them the more he became convinced he was right. His gaydar rarely failed him. He wanted desperately to know if Tuck had said anything about Brian and him to Jeff, after Jeff told his dad he was gay, but it was something even in his brashness he could never ask. Michael had no idea that Jeff knew also, and it was something Jeff would never tell, as long as his fathers wanted the secret kept.

Before he hung up on Michael, Jeff heard Jerry mumble in the background, "Is everything OK?"

Aha!!!! So Jerry was at Michael's apartment. Hallelujah!!!

On the way to the barbeque, Jim and Jeff stopped at a Walmart and bought a small gift for Amy, Mackenzie's daughter. When they got to the barbeque in Brian's back yard, everyone else was there. The two fathers were lying on the grass playing with Amy. They were cooing and tickling her like the two doting grandfathers they were, and little Amy was obliging them by giggling.

When Mackenzie saw her 'brother' she ran over, threw her arms around Jeff, and said, "I am so sorry about you and Marie."

"Don't be," He answered. "It was over a long time ago."

"And who's this handsome specimen?" she turned her attention to Jim.

Without hesitation, Jeff took Jim's hand and with the widest grin he could muster, he said, "Mackenzie, this is Jim Lester. He's my new business associate and my life partner. My folks already know."

It really took a while for that statement to process through Mackenzie's brain. There are no words to describe how shocked she was. To her credit she was able to recover rather quickly. Again she threw her arms around Jeff, and muttered in his ear, "I'm so happy for you. I'll always love you." Then she turned to Jim. "Well all I can say is that I now have two extremely handsome brothers." She embraced Jim and kissed him on the cheek.

"You'd better tell my folks and my husband so we can get back to the barbeque. Actually, I'm starved."

Tuck and Brian had already handed Amy over to Peter, and they had rejoined their wives. Mackenzie walked Jeff over to her parents with Jim following closely. Then she motioned Peter to come over and join them. Tuck and Maryann were viewing the scene from a short distance away. At one point Tuck could see Brian's knees buckle and Jeff grab his arm to keep him from falling. Colleen's mouth was hanging open, and Peter was staring in disbelief.

Peter made the first move. He offered Jim his hand and put his other hand on Jim's shoulder. It was obvious he was congratulating him. Then he did the same to Jeff. Finally Colleen, reaching high, put her arms around Jeff's neck and pulled him down for a big wet kiss on his cheek. Then Jim got the same treatment.

Brian just stood there, unable to move. Jeff went over to him. "Aren't you going to wish me luck, godfather," he said imitating Marlon Brando. This broke Brian's trance, and he started to laugh, grabbed Jeff in a bear hug, and kissed him on both cheeks. He didn't have to say a word. With that bear hug he was telling Jeff, that it was OK with him. He broke away from Jeff, and extended his hand to Jim, and then embraced him as well.

"Now can we eat?" Mackenzie begged.

The barbeque was a huge success. Everyone was truly relaxed and comfortable and they could see how happy their beloved Jeffrey was. That was enough for all of them. They all hovered around Jim trying to get to know him better. Of course, he charmed them all. Even Amy was delighted with the stuffed animal the guys had given her. She was not treating it well, and it was obvious it would soon be a goner.

Somehow during the festivities, Tuck got a second alone with Brian. He whispered in his ear that the boys knew about them, and he would tell him all about it when they were alone. For a moment Brian turned white and looked like he was going to pass out again. But suddenly he brightened up.

"I'm glad," he said to Tuck. "Finally someone, no, some ones, we can confide in. Isn't that wonderful?"

Tuck thought about that. All these years they had held their secret all to themselves, and now they could actually talk about it to someone, openly and freely. It was an unexpected reaction from the two fathers. RELIEF!

"Let's make a date to get together with the boys on one of our boy's nights out." Tuck said. We need to talk to someone and let it out of our systems." He was so elated he started to hyperventilate. "We'll arrange it at the gym tomorrow."

"Roger," Brian agreed

Tucker and Brian used sporting events as an excuse to get out of the house together. They would take a room at a motel that rented by the hour, making sure to be back at the arena for the end of the event. They also used the motel when they were able to take a long lunch hour at work, and they even had sex in the locker room at their gym when nobody was around. Their favorite outing was a fishing trip together. They had learned to be very resourceful.

Brian and Tuck had basketball tickets for Thursday evening. Tuck called Jeff at work on Monday morning and asked if he and Jim were free that Thursday evening. Jeff said he was sure they were. Tuck asked if he and Jim would join Brian and him at the basketball game on Thursday if he could get two more tickets.

"Sounds like fun," Jeff answered.

"I'll call you back as soon as I know," he told Jeff and hung up. He then called the arena and secured two seats three rows behind his and Brian's seats. He suddenly realized that he and Brian would be giving up a sport night sex session, but it was worth it.

He called back and arranged to pick up his 'sons' at their condo at 6:00 PM. It was on their way to the arena, and it would give them time to have dinner before the game.

"Great Dad," Jeff said. I'm really looking forward to it. Jeff was thrilled to be doing something again with his dad. It had been years since they had gone to a game together. But why was there a stirring in his groin?

At the appointed time, Brian and Tuck picked the boys up. They had been waiting in the lobby where Jeff had first met Mrs. Crane and where he had wondered if anybody ever used this beautiful lobby. They climbed into the back seat of Tuck's car and headed to the arena. Tuck used valet parking so they wouldn't have to walk from the far end of the parking lot. They picked up the two extra tickets at the will call window, and went into the arena. There was plenty of fast food available, but there was also a small restaurant for a better meal. Tuck led them all to the restaurant.

Brian and Tuck ordered baked salmon and Jim and Jeff ordered a porterhouse steak to share. Conversation remained light and no one brought up the real reason for the meeting, and during the game there were no opportunities to talk at all. During the half time break, being as astute as he was, Jeff pulled his father aside and asked if he and Brian wanted to unburden a little.

"Oh God, yes," Tuck said. "I just didn't know how to begin."

"Why don't you guys come up to our place after the game? I'll make coffee and we'll talk."

"I think we've had enough of the subterfuge. Let's beat the crowd and get to your place now," Tuck pleaded.

When they arrived at the condo, Jim guided them to guest parking and they parked in the exact same space that Jeff had parked just a few short days ago. They made their way up to the condo, and Jim showed them around the place.

"Beautiful view of the city," Brian said as they all sat down in the living room and made themselves comfortable. Jeff offered them something harder than coffee, but they declined, so Jim went into the kitchen and put up the coffee. After examining the contents of the fridge he asked everyone if toasted English muffins would be OK.

"Fine." Everyone said at once.

Jeff set the dining room table and noticed that his fathers were fidgety and visually uncomfortable.

"Are you OK, Dad?" he asked.

"Yes, but there is so much Brian and I want to tell you, hopefully to make you understand. But I just don't know where to start."

"It's always a good idea to start at the beginning."

They waited until Jeff finished setting the table and Jim returned from the kitchen. They all got comfortable again in the living room, and Tuck started first. He quickly described how Brian and he met at work on their very first day.

Brian continued: "When I first looked at your father's face that first day at work, something came over me that I can't explain to this day. He was drop dead handsome. My heart skipped a beat. I knew that I wanted to know this man. It never occurred to me then that it could be sexual." Jeff and Jim exchanged knowing glances.

Then Tuck added, "On the plane to our corporate orientation in St. Louis, we sat together. Our knees and arms kept touching and neither of us pulled away. I wanted to feel him, and believe me I was confused." He looked at the boys unable to say another word.

"Please," Jeff said. "You can certainly tell us. Our story is not much different. The only thing we would change is the circumstances." Tuck was reassured and he continued.

"We arrived at the hotel late in the day and only had a little over an hour to shower, change and meet the other interns for dinner. To save time, we showered together. I think we knew what would happen and we both wanted it." He looked at Brian, smiled and reached for his hand.

Tuck continued. He explained about the pact they made never to hurt their wives, and to keep their love a deep secret. He described how they would arrange business trips, long lunches, sport nights when they really didn't go to the game until it was nearly over, fishing trips and so on.

"It's been a constant battle of deception, son," he said. "I'm not proud of it. But Brian and I have to assure you that we have never let our wives suffer. We have been good and loving husbands and fathers, in and out of the bedroom." That last statement made Jeff definitely uncomfortable.

"If you hadn't discovered us," Tuck continued, "we would still be living the secret with nobody to talk to. You don't know what a relief it is to be able to tell someone how much I love Brian and he loves me." Tuck lowered his head and started to cry. That got Brian crying too. Jeff got up and put his arms around his father to console him. Jim did the same to Brian.

It was time for a break so they went to the dining room for their coffee and muffins. At the table, Jim and Jeff related their story. True, the circumstances were different, but the emotions were the same and every time one of them could manage to describe an emotion in words, the others nodded in agreement.

"Hey guys," Tuck said. "Brian and I are going on our semi annual weekend fishing trip, er, I mean, non fishing trip, next month. The cabin we rent has two bedrooms. It would be great if you could join us. It's a real nature weekend. We usually hang out in the buff, but if that would make you uncomfortable, we can make it clothing optional."

Jim and Jeff looked at each other. They really weren't sure if it was a good idea or not. Jeff caught Tuck looking at him pleadingly.

Tuck implored Jim and Jeff. "You know kids, for better or worse, we have a different relationship now than we had just a few days ago. I have a feeling it's going to be a much closer relationship. Let's start the bonding of the new relationship. Please say, yes, you'll join us on our trip."

CHAPTER SEVEN

Brian and Tuck drove to their sons' condo on a warm, sunny Friday morning. They all had arranged to take a very long weekend off, Friday to Monday. They were going 'fishing' and had rented a rustic lodge on a beautiful lake about two hour's drive from the city. It was where Tuck and Brian had spent many an idyllic weekend in the past. Tuck had told Jim and Jeff that the cabin was very isolated, very private and that the nearest other cabin was about a mile away.

As they were packing, Jim joked to Jeff that Brian and Tuck were living out 'Brokeback Mountain' except that they weren't cowboys. Jeff agreed that it sure seemed that way.

The sons hopped into the middle seats of Tucks' van, and Jeff unceremoniously announced that they hadn't had breakfast yet.

"Neither have we," Brian informed them "so let's look for a place to stop."

"There's a Denny's about four blocks up from here," Jim told Tuck. "Let's stop there."

They all decided 'what the hell!' They were on vacation and so they all ordered super grand slams. They finished every bite, were surprised at themselves and congratulated one another amidst hearty laughter. Brian picked up the check and Jeff objected.

"Listen squirt," Tuck jokingly put down his son. "This trip's on your old man, make that, your two old men, so you two can just retire your wallets, and I don't want to hear another word about it."

"It works for me." Jim answered for Jeff and him.

Back in the car there were no awkward periods of silence. They talked about anything and everything. They talked about the home team's chances to reach the playoffs, their work, their sex lives (but nothing embarrassing, just some amusing incidents), the probability that Jim's and Jeff's mutual friend, Michael, and Jim's college room mate, Jerry, might be starting something beautiful, etc., etc. Conversation between them was easy, and never forced. They were more like old, long time friends, than fathers and sons. They reached the cabin in what seemed to them, no time at all.

The four men unloaded the car and brought their gear, including fishing gear they would never use, into the cabin. They entered into a very large living/dining room, fully furnished. The dining room opened into a fair sized kitchen. There was a circuit breaker box in the kitchen. Brian went over to the box and flicked the circuits to the on position. The refrigerator began to hum. There were two doors off one side of the living room which led to the two bedrooms. Also off the living room was a small hallway, which led to a tiny bathroom, and off the dining room there were sliding glass doors which led to a small porch facing the lake. The porch had a love seat, a coffee table and two easy chairs, one on each side of the love seat.

"This is perfect," Jeff said, and Jim agreed.

Tuck had brought a case of beer with them and he said, "Let's get the beer into the fridge, and hang up our clothes. Then let's go down to the store and buy some food."

They had each packed plenty of camping clothes for the weekend. "I don't know about you fellers," Tuck said to his sons, "but Brian and I won't be wearing much of this stuff anyway."

"We always use the bedroom on the left," Tuck said. He picked up his bag and headed that way. Brian followed him, and they closed the door. Jeff and Jim could not help but smile. They went to their room, hung up their clothes and put whatever had to be put in drawers into the small dresser. They gave each other yet another good morning kiss, and went back into the living room.

Their dads' door was still closed, so Jeff banged on it and yelled, "Hey guys, you'll have plenty of time for that later. Now we're going shopping."

The door opened and two fully dressed, red faced, middle aged men, came out, obviously very erect. All four of them started to laugh, but managed to contain themselves long enough to get back into the car. Each one thought to himself how amazing it was that there was no embarrassment between them. They were all with their lovers and boners were apt to happen. So what?

Tuck drove about two miles and they came upon a small cluster of stores. It was hardly a town. One of the stores was an old fashioned general store.

"Here we are," Tuck said and parked in front of the shop. They went in, and Brian and Tucker headed for the refrigerator section to get butter, milk, eggs, and orange juice. They also purchased bread, jam, ketchup, hamburger meat, buns, a few hefty steaks, and a variety of other necessities. The next stop was the freezer section, where they picked out frozen French fries, and an assortment of frozen vegetables.

Jim and Jeff, on the other hand, were acting like a couple of kids. They were running around the store picking up potato chips, pop corn, candy bars and other snacks.

The shop owner's son was at the cash register. All four of the visitors began to drool. He was drop dead gorgeous. He stood six feet tall. There was not an ounce of fat on him. His shirt barely contained his bulging muscles and rippled chest. They stared at his steel blue eyes as he asked, "You folks visiting out here?"

"Yup," Tuck answered, and told him where they were staying.

"Too bad," the hunk said. "The fishing's not really so good at that spot. You'd be better off about a mile further up the lake."

"We'll be fine," Jeff said, just so he could talk to Mr. America. "We're just here for the rest and relaxation this place offers us."

"Yes," the young man agreed. "It's always great to get away from the hustle and bustle of the city. I come here every weekend and help my folks out in the store. It relaxes me and gives my folks a break." His smile was so infectious that Jeff was prompted to get friendlier.

He stuck out his hand and said, "I'm Jeff Simmons, this is my dad, Tucker and my godfather, Brian O'Toole." Then with a flourish and no hesitation at all, he put his arm around Jim's shoulder and said, "And this Greek Adonis is my partner, Jim Lester." He waited for a reaction from the hunk but all he got was an extended hand. When their hands met, the hunk said, "I'm Ron Fisher. It's a pleasure to meet you folks."

"Where do you work in the city?" Jim asked. He really wanted to know. This guy could be a friend.

"I'm an investment advisor," he said. "I just recently went out on my own, and rented space at 200 North Elm, downtown," he informed them.

"I don't believe it," Jeff said. "We're right across the street at 201. One of my best friends, and my college roommate, is in your building. He's an attorney, Michael Costello."

Ron tossed his head back and looked at Jeff in disbelief. "You've got to be kidding. Michael's my lawyer. My partner referred him to me (uh oh, what kind of partner?) Michael just got me my incorporation papers, registered my name and all that other legal stuff for domestic partners. (Question answered) Wait a minute." He took his wallet out of his pocket and fumbled around for a card. "He also suggested I get an accountant before I screw things up. I've got his card right here, and he's in your building. Maybe you know him?" He looked at the card and burst out laughing. "It's you," he said. "This is beyond belief. I am so happy to have met you guys, and I promise, Jeff, I'll call for an appointment Monday morning."

"Make that Tuesday," Jeff said. "We're booked here until Monday evening.

"That's a deal," Ron said and he could not stop smiling. Jeff, ever the business man, was thinking that an investment advisor was another great source for business referrals. The same thought went through Jim's mind.

Just then another handsome, well built guy came into the store. Brian and Tucker, Jeff and Jim were really beginning to enjoy all the eye candy this place had to offer. The young man had jet black hair, soft brown eyes and the squarest jaw any of them had ever seen. He went right over to Ron and without regard to the assembled masses, he smacked one wet kiss on Ron's lips.

"Hey men," Ron said. I'd like you to meet my partner, Foster Grant, and don't laugh please. He's not related to the sunglass people." He then introduced Foster to everybody, and added, "Foster, Michael Costello was Jeff's college roommate and they're good friends. Can you believe it?"

"That's incredible," Foster said. "We've all got to get together in the city, and really get to know each other. Too bad Michael is single."

"I wouldn't be so sure of it, guys. I recently introduced him to my college roommate, Jerry, and things seem to be progressing quite nicely," Jim informed them.

Ron and Foster muttered together, "No shit!" Then Foster added, "I thought he was a confirmed slut and bachelor."

Although they were enjoying the banter, Brian and Tucker were anxious to get back to the cabin and have sex. It had been a while since they had been able to steal away together.

"This is great guys, but we old folks would like to get back to the cabin. We need our 'rest and relaxation' more than you young uns," he said jokingly with a raised eyebrow. He and Brian gathered up the groceries and put them in the car while the young dudes said their goodbyes, exchanged business cards and promised to get together in the city. Jeff noticed that Foster was an architect. He also realized that his and Jim's circle of gay friends was increasing. He had heard that gays created their own gay families and he could see it happening to them.

Back at the cabin, they put away the groceries and refrigerated the perishables. Then, without any embarrassment, Tuck grabbed Brian around the waist and said, "Look guys, we are as horny as hell, so please just excuse us." He hustled Brian into the bedroom and closed the door.

The cabin was great, but insulated it was not. The beds creaked very loudly and every word spoken could be heard anywhere in the cabin. Jeff and Jim had seated themselves on the sofa in the living room and were making out a little, but they could hear the bed creaking and then were serenaded to: Suck that cock, baby. Suck harder, my love. Stop before I come, hon. Etcetera. Sometimes the words were spoken by Brian and sometimes by Tuck. It was silent for a bit and then they heard Brian say, "Drive it home, sweetheart. Make baby happy." And then the bed started to creak loudly. Brian and Tuck were aware of the noise they were making, but neither gave a damn.

All of this was too much for Jeff and Jim. Before they knew what hit them, they were fully disrobed, and lying on the couch in a 69 position. They were so hot they couldn't take the time to go to the bedroom. They sucked each other's cocks for a while, and then they moved down to the floor, which had a not so soft area rug. They didn't even notice how hard the floor was. They were too far gone in sexual ecstasy. There was no lube handy, so Jeff spit on his hand and wet his cock. Between his saliva and Jim's, he felt secure enough to enter Jim's waiting love receptacle. Jim had turned on his back in full preparation and expectation of the joy to come. Jeff entered Jim easily. They both marveled at how much easier it was getting for them to enter each other. They both murmured softly as the pleasure they were giving each other increased. Jeff could hold back no longer and he came with a muffled shriek.

It was not muffled enough. Tuck was fucking Brian when they heard the scream. That scream meant only one thing, and the two fathers smiled and went back to pleasing one another.

Tuck said, "They must be on the living room floor, or else we would have heard the bed creak long ago."

After Jeff came, he and Jim rested a while and switched positions. Needless to say the two young studs came long before their dads. It would take a while before they would learn how to delay their climaxes. After Jim came, they fell asleep in each other's arms on the hard living room floor. There was no mess. Their cum was well buried in their rectums.

They were so deep in sleep, they didn't hear their dads' screeches when each of them came, and these two guys screamed out, not holding back, in their new found freedom. Unlike their sons they were covered with cum. The bathroom was in the hall. They stealthily opened the door and saw the two young studs sound asleep on the floor. They looked like two angels and the dads smiled in contentment. As quietly as possible they crept to the bathroom and cleaned up.

On the way back to their room, they stood over the sleeping beauties and admired their handsome bodies. There was enough room on each side of the boys for another body to join them. They read each other's minds and Tuck lay down next to his son and Brian lay down next to Jim. The older men hunkered up to their kids, and they too fell asleep.

In his sleep, Tuck was aware that he was sleeping with a man and not Maryann. He knew it wasn't Brian. The body next to him was harder and more muscular than Brian. His muscle memory sent his arm around his companion's waist and down his abdomen, coming gently to rest on the limp cock. In his sleep he began to stroke the dream cock and it began to harden. The sleeping body turned toward Tuck and thrust his cock forward. The two cocks met, kissed and rubbed against each other. Both pricks were rock hard. It's amazing how real a dream can be.

The two ethereal faces were an inch apart and getting closer. Their lips met and began to kiss. Their lips parted and their tongues gently joined. Their hands groped one another's body seeking the wonder of all wonders, their love tools. How good this felt. Real love was taking over from lust and pure sex. In their sleep, each body thought, "I love this man. I need him so badly."

In years to come they would not be able to tell you who started to wake up first, but awaken they did. Jeff was the first to be aware of what was happening. He made no attempt to pull away. All he could think of was, "It's my fantasy. It's coming true."

He pulled Tuck closer to him and held him so tight that he knew his dad could not pull away. Now Tuck was also entering into the sphere of awareness. He wanted to speak but Jeff was kissing him so hard he could not.

He was so far gone by this time, he couldn't have stopped the love making if he wanted to.

"Fuck me dad, please. I'm begging you," Jeff pleaded.

Tuck was in a stupor. He wasn't thinking clearly. He thought that Jeff sounded tortured. If he didn't do what Jeff wanted, surely his son would die. Jeff turned on his back, and Tuck entered him without any lubrication. It hurt Jeff for a moment, but he didn't care. His father could have fucked him with a baseball bat and he wouldn't have cared.

It was as if they had been doing this all their lives, that's how easily they found a gentle, steady rhythm. They began to moan softly as Tuck leaned forward and kissed his son. Tuck's fingers found Jeff's nipples and he began to pinch them sensuously.

Jeff whispered in his dad's ear, "I have dreamed of this moment ever since I saw you fucking Brian. Thank you for making my dream come true. I don't give a rat's fuck what society would think of this. For you and me it's right."

"I know son. I feel it's right too. I just hope those two sleeping beauties agree. I love Brian so much, I hurt when I think of him," he whispered back, as he felt his climax drawing nearer. Jeff was about to cum too as his dad's cock rubbed gently against his prostate.

Their moaning grew louder as their orgasms approached. Brian and Jim began to stir. They awoke to find themselves wrapped up together, as the two men lying next to them climaxed simultaneously with the loudest screams they ever heard.

"What the fuck?" Jim yelled out. He was shocked, but he wasn't angry. He knew what Jeff's fantasy was and he really didn't mind. Jeff's own father was no threat to him or to Jeff's love for him. Besides, he was positive that Tuck and Brian were soul mates, as were he and Jeff.

Tuck rolled off Jeff and sat up. There wasn't room for him to lie next to Brian. The sofa was in the way, so he gently lowered himself on Brian's torso and began to kiss him so lovingly that Brian melted under him. Now Jeff could roll over to Jim and he started to say something, but Jim put his finger on Jeff's lips indicating that no words were necessary.

They lay that way for a while, the two couples wrapped up in each other's arms and in each other's love until Brian said, "It's not fair, Tuck, that you could enjoy such young cock and leave me out of it."

With that, he pushed Tuck off of him and grabbed Jim's cock.

"Wow," he said in a mock voice. "Young cock feels so much better than old cock." When he had grabbed Jim's cock, Jeff separated from Jim to give Brian more room so Brian took advantage of the situation and went down on Jim. The events of the last half hour had so excited Jim that he came almost instantly, which caused Brian to laugh.

"I take it back," he said. "Old cock lasts longer than young cock. That was way too fast, young man. I hardly had a chance to enjoy you." He then added as an afterthought, "But you do taste mighty good."

With that Jim went down on Brian and Jeff went down on his father. Then it got really wild. They kept switching partners and positions until none of them was aware of who was doing what to whom. At some point Jim and Jeff came again, but Brian and Tuck had it for now.

Eventually Tuck asked, "Has anyone noticed how hard this floor is?" Everyone got up and decided it was time to clean up. They showered one at a time. The shower was too small for more than one person. They had missed lunch altogether, and it was time to start thinking about making dinner.

"Steaks or burgers?" Tuck asked

Brian said, "I've got an idea. Let's see if Ron and Foster are available to join us, and if they are we can make both and share."

Jeff went into his bedroom, reached into his wallet, and found Ron's business card. Fortunately his cell number was on it. Ron answered after the first ring. He thought that it was a generous invitation, asked Jeff to hold a minute while he talked to Foster, and then they accepted.

"Be here around six," Jeff told him. He hung up the phone, turned to his family and said, "We need to set up for six, and then we have to get dressed."

CHAPTER EIGHT

Ron and Foster arrived promptly at 6 PM. Ron remembered that the men had purchased steaks and ground beef, and he rightly assumed that was what they would have for dinner, so he decided to bring two bottles of red wine. They were both wearing tank tops, cut off denim short shorts, and sandals. From the contour of their crotches, Jim was sure that they were not wearing any underwear.

The beef was formed into patties and was already in the broiler. The steaks were waiting on top of the outdoor barbeque. Two of the canned vegetables were now in pots, warming slowly on the stove. The frozen fries were slowly frying in vegetable oil in a deep frying pan. Tuck went to look for wine glasses but there weren't any so he put out juice glasses. It would have to do. Brian asked how everyone would like their steaks. He, Tuck and Jeff passed, saying the hamburgers would be enough. Jim, Ron and Foster all wanted their steaks medium rare. Jeff then seasoned the steaks and lit the barbeque.

Jeff and Jim said they would get the meal ready and suggested everyone else get out of the kitchen, sit on the porch and watch the setting sun. That was fine with everyone, and those who were not on kitchen duty went outside.

Tuck stayed behind and retrieved four beers from the fridge and brought them outside for the others to enjoy.

On the porch, conversation was a little stiff. Ron and Foster assumed that the fathers were straight and they didn't feel totally free to be themselves. Brian, bless his soul, figured it out immediately, and tried to find a way to put the boys at ease.

So just like that, he asked, "How long have you guys been together, and how did you meet?"

"We've been together about five years. But let's wait to tell how we met until we're at dinner. I want to hear how Jeff and Jim met also," Foster said, and then Ron added, "and I want to hear about Jim's college room mate, Jerry, who has apparently stolen Michael's heart."

In the kitchen, Jeff and Jim put the cooked hamburgers on one platter, and the fries on another. They put the two veggies in bowls with serving spoons. There was no relish, but they put out a bottle of ketchup, and salt and pepper. They also put out some more beer and the two bottles of wine. When the steaks were almost ready, Jim called the guys in for dinner.

Everybody filled their plates, and Jim put the steaks on a platter for the three men who wanted them. They started to eat in silence, but finally Brian said to Ron and Foster, "Okay, so tell us how you two guys met."

Ron smiled at Foster and began. We were both seniors in college. I was attending Georgetown in DC and Foster was going to Emory in Atlanta. It was spring break time and both of us went down to Ft. Lauderdale. My buddies were all out on the prowl looking for pussy, but I had other ideas. I checked the gay yellow pages, and headed for a gay bar in the gay section of town. I got there and was ready to leave after a few minutes because the disco music was deafening. I was just finishing my one and only drink and turned to leave, when I felt someone put his hand on my shoulder and ask, 'Would you like to dance?' It was Foster of course. I took one look at him and asked, 'Why waste time? Can we get right to the sex?' You should have seen the look on his face."

Foster continued. "I grabbed Ron's hand and dragged him outside where we could hear each other talk. I asked him if he was serious and he assured me he was. I told him that my grandparents owned a condo in Pompano Beach, only a short drive from there. I let him know that they were up north until next October, and I was using the condo all by myself. Ron had come by taxi, but I had use of grandpa's car, so off we went.

"When we got into the condo," Foster continued, "I hardly had time to lock the door and Ron was all over me. We must have stood in the hallway for ten minutes, kissing, sucking tongue and groping our packages."

He suddenly stopped and looked at the two fathers. "I'm really sorry Mr. Simmons, Mr. O'Toole. "If this offends you, I can stop the story."

"Nonsense," Brian said. "You can be perfectly candid with us, even as regards the sordid details," he said, raising his eyebrows in a leering fashion.

Foster wasn't quite convinced and Ron took over. "We finally let go of each other, stripped quicker than the speed of a speeding bullet, and climbed into bed. I will skip the 'sordid details' but I can tell you it was the best night of my life up to then."

"The next morning we went over to my motel. I checked out, moved into the condo, and we spent the rest of spring break together. By the end of the week there was no doubt in either of our minds that we would be together for life. Thank God, we were both graduating in a few weeks. Our phone bills were bankrupting us. We would sit at our computers and IM each other for hours and then call one another and talk for hours more." Ron stopped to breathe. He took Foster's hand in his and held it gently. There was a tear in his eye.

"We are a team forever," he said.

Foster continued the narrative. "Anyway, independently we researched the best city to begin a career in our respective fields, and came up with Phoenix. We started sending resumees to names in the telephone book and we both landed good jobs, but now with nearly five years experience, we are both striking out on our own. It's really scary. By the way," he looked at his new friends, "that's how I met Michael. He was counsel for my firm. The first day I met him, he told me he was taking me out to lunch and he hit on me. I cut his desire short, but we became really good friends."

Jim said, "It was easy for you guys. You met in a gay bar and knew how you stood immediately. Jeff and I each lived with a gay guy for four years thinking we were straight. The only similarity between us is that the moment I shook Jeff's hand, I knew where my life was going. I fell for him, hook, line and sinker."

"Me too," Jeff answered. As he said that, he stood up, went to Jim, wrapped his arms around Jim's shoulders from the rear, and kissed his neck. Ron and Foster started to applaud, and Brian and Tucker started to cry. Ron thought, 'These guys have such understanding fathers. How great is that?'

Tuck said, "We'll clean up after you guys leave. It's such a beautiful night. Let's go outside."

They took two extra chairs outside and sat on the back porch enjoying the evening breeze and sipping beer. They looked like a bunch of kids at summer camp sitting around the campfire (except for the beer.) They chewed the fat, telling amusing stories as they occurred to them. A casual observer would have thought that they had known each other for a hundred years.

Finally Ron said that it was time to go. He had to open the store early tomorrow morning, but they would have Sunday off. Tuck wanted to ask them back for tomorrow evening and maybe Sunday, but he suddenly realized that Ron's and Foster's presence would interfere in their sex lives. He just embraced both boys in a bear hug, then Brian did the same. The four out gay men, kissed on the lips as they hugged each other.

The moment was a little awkward until Jim said, "If we don't see you before we leave, we will definitely get together in the city. Hey, I've got a great idea. Michael doesn't know we've met. Jeff and I will make a date with him and Jerry, if they are still together, and you two can casually waltz in."

"Fantastic idea," Foster said. "We'll give him another six degrees of separation story or maybe more like two degrees."

Ron and Foster said goodbye once again, and told the guys what a great time they had, at least six times before they finally left.

They all pitched in cleaning up from dinner, and the cabin was ship shape in no time. They were very tired and decided to turn in.

Tuck yawned and said, "I've had it, and no offense, my dear sons, but I want to be alone with my love tonight. OK?"

"No sweat," Jeff answered. "I think my love would like a private session with me too."

The four men kissed each other goodnight. The kisses were far from fatherly, nor were they sexually inviting either. They were just pecks on the cheek like four gay men usually implant upon each other when they say hello or goodbye.

Once the guys got into bed, the slightest noise in either room could be heard clearly by the occupants of the other room. Brian and Tuck began making the noises of love as they had earlier in the day. Jeff began to laugh and yelled out, "I bet you brought us to this place on purpose to embarrass us, but I for one intend to ignore the sounds you two are making."

"Likewise," Brian yelled out and everyone could hear Tuck laughing from the pit of his belly. He and Brian agreed that this was the best 'fishing' weekend of their lives.

Ron drove his car home. He laid his hand on Foster's knee, and Foster automatically spread his legs. Ron spoke first.

"Did you see what I saw?" he asked Foster.

Foster: "That depends. What did you see?"

Ron: "When we were going out on the porch before dinner, and Tuck went to get the beer, I just happened to glance back. He pinched Jeff on his ass as he went by him. Also, when we were all out on the porch after dinner, occasionally Tuck put his hand on Brian's thigh just as I'm doing to you now."

Foster: "So what does that prove?"

Ron: "Nothing except that it was very clear to me that Brian had a boner, and it was big,"

Foster: "I married a fucking crotch watcher. Listen, I don't want to jeopardize our new friendship with Jim and Jeff, so please keep your suspicions to yourself. Let's not be the one to out Jeff's fathers, even if Jim and Jeff may be privy to the situation."

"You can count on it, babe," Ron assured Foster.

It's amazing how Brian and Tuck could deceive the entire straight world, and every gay man who met them saw the truth of their love, one, two, three.

Back at the cabin a symphony was playing. In one room Brian and Tuck were moaning, groaning and cumming with ecstatic screams. It didn't seem to bother them that Jim and Jeff could hear every word. Jim and Jeff on the other hand were totally distracted. Every time they heard those love noises they started to giggle so hard they couldn't concentrate on sex. At one point, Jim had his head buried in Jeff's crotch, when Brian gave such a large moan of pure joy, that Jim started to laugh so hard he nearly bit Jeff's cock off. They finally decided that it was a losing game and just cuddled until they fell asleep. Sex would have to wait.

The boys were awakened by the smell of bacon frying. They both had to pee so they got out of bed sporting enormous woodies and headed for the bathroom. They were naked, but that seemed to be the uniform of the day. On the way they had to go through the living room and they could view the kitchen. Brian was cooking and Tuck was setting the table.

"Good morning," four voices said at once.

Tuck asked, "How about going skinny dipping with us after breakfast? It's the best exercise I can think of since Brian and I can't go to the gym."

"You're on," Jim said. It will have to replace our morning run."

He and Jeff went to the bathroom and crossed swords. They managed to brush their teeth and wash their faces together, but it was a tight fit.

Brian and Tuck were naked so the boys joined them at the kitchen table as naked as the day they were born. Brian served up a generous portion of bacon and eggs with white toast which he had already buttered. Very little was said, but finally Tuck asked, "Are you guys all right with our little romp of yesterday?"

Jeff and Jim looked at each other not knowing what to say. Jim knew that the ball was his to run with. He smiled at Jeff, took his hand, turned to Brian and Tucker and said, "We are not only all right with it but in fact, a repeat performance would be perfectly welcome. I gotta tell you, it was fun."

Brian and Tucker looked so, so relieved, as did Jeff. The subject was dropped and nothing more was said about it. After breakfast, they washed the dishes, pots and pans in the sink. There was no dishwasher in the cabin. They grabbed some towels and a blanket and ran bare ass down to the lake. They spread out the blanket on the grass, threw the towels on it and headed for the water.

Once submerged, they began to play grab ass. Nobody really knew who was grabbing whose ass or cock, but they were all having fun. At one point, Jim enveloped Jeff in his arms, leaving Tuck to Brian. A little later Jeff looked over to see his fathers pressed together like two spoons. Brian was in the back and Tucker was moaning like a banshee.

"Goddamn," Jeff said to Jim. "Brian is fucking my dad. I've got an idea." He swam over and got his front against Brian's back. He positioned his cock in Brian's crack and entered slowly. Brian winced a bit and then began to moan in sheer joy. Not to be outdone, Jim placed his back against Tuck's front and guided Tuck's cock into him. Talking stopped, moaning began. The moans got louder and louder and bingo, one after the other they shot their loads. Jim's cum fed the fishes. The other's deposited their juices in someone's warm receptacle.

Spent, they got out of the water, toweled dried themselves, and lay down on the blanket. They got as close as they could to each other. Their arms and legs interwoven like delicate lace. It was hard to tell which limb belonged to whom. They fell asleep in the morning sun and slept for two hours.

The rest of the day, they had sex with each other in every combination. When Jeff and Tuck were making love it was particularly erotic for both of them, but when the partners were making love it was just comforting knowing that they belonged together, and would continue to belong together for a lifetime. The four of them had bonded together in love, joy, and comfort.

At about 4 PM they all fell asleep, but at 5 PM Jeff's cell phone rang shrilly and woke them up. It was Ron.

"Hi Jeff," he said. You guys were so gracious last night that Foster and I would like to take you all out to dinner tonight. There's a great barbeque joint not far from here called 'Joey's Place.' It's very informal. You can wear shorts."

Jeff said, "It sounds great to me. How about we pick you guys up in my dad's van at about 6:30?"

"Perfect," Ron answered. "See you then."

Jeff hung up and roused the others. Again they were forced to shower individually, and it took a while for everyone to get ready for the evening. The fathers wore shorts, tee shirts and sandals, and looked like their sons' brothers. The sons wore shorts, tank tops and sandals. Every one of them looked really hot, and would catch a few eyes for sure, male and female.

Ron and Foster were wearing shorts also, but not as short as the evening before. They completed their outfits with tank tops and sandals. They all looked great, but Ron's muscles, barely contained by the tank top, took the evening's grand prize. He and Foster climbed into the middle seats of the van. Jim and Jeff were already in the rear. Under Ron's direction, they started for the restaurant.

CHAPTER NINE

It was another great evening for the extended family. The restaurant was warm and friendly. The staff and the other customers could not take their eyes off the six gorgeous hunks as they were seated. And that goes for the fathers too. All those mornings at the gym had paid off. They were trim, muscular, and healthy. They looked like older brothers to the four young men. Nobody would guess they were the fathers.

Brian and Tuck ordered a combo of barbequed chicken and ribs. The others ordered a full rack of ribs. The side dishes were served family style, and all you can eat. The waiter placed bowl after bowl on the table. There was corn on the cob, mashed potatoes, French fries, sweet potato fries, peas, green beans, and finally corn on the cob. Tuck realized that there were no 'healthy' vegetables on the table. He was all right with it. This weekend, anything goes.

They all ate with gusto amid much laughter and joking. Their vibes spread throughout the restaurant, and suddenly the waiter came by with a round of tap beer in a huge pitcher. He pointed to an elderly couple across the room and said, "Compliments of the Smiths, over there." The six men raised their glasses as a thank you and a salute.

Tuck leaned over and whispered in Brian's ear, "This is so great, to be allowed to be who we are. His cheek was wet from an errant tear. I wish we could do it more often." Brian nodded his head trying not to cry as well.

Suddenly Tuck had an epiphany. All these years, he and Brian had never been short on gay sex. They satisfied themselves often enough. It was the emotional side of gay life that had been denied them. The good gay friends to socialize with, the camaraderie, these had all slipped by them. He would share that thought with his beloved Brian, when they were alone.

With that thought in mind, Tuck decided that good times with good friends might be even more important than sex. The idea of that surprised him, but he put that thought aside. He asked Ron what time he was leaving tomorrow.

"About 6 PM," he said. "That will get us home about 8 or 8:30, depending on traffic, and we can get a good night's rest before the rigors of a Monday morning set in."

"Good," Tuck said. "Come over tomorrow. Have breakfast with us and then join us skinny dipping in the lake."

Now Ron was certain Tuck and Brian were gay. He consulted briefly with Foster and they accepted.

"That's great," Tuck smiled at Ron, but you better bring some extra bacon and eggs. I think we used most of it this morning."

Ron laughed. "It's a done deal," he said.

The next morning, Jim and Jeff rose early. Once again the noises coming from the fathers' room kept them awake and giggling. Jim got the frying pans ready and Jeff set the table for six. They were wearing their boxer shorts. They didn't want to shock Ron and Foster when they arrived.

When they did arrive, Brian and Tucker were still in the bedroom. Jeff shouted, "Company's here. Get decent and come get your breakfast." Their warning fell on deaf ears. Brian and Tucker darted out of the bedroom and ran to the bathroom wearing nothing at all. It was obvious to the young men that they were carrying morning woodies with them. Ron and Foster wondered if they were indeed morning woodies or something else was going on. They both marveled at the breadth of Brian's cock.

As I said, you could hear every noise in the cabin. The men could hear the fathers peeing, brushing their teeth and washing up. Then they darted out of the bathroom and back to their bedroom. Their cocks were flaccid. When they emerged they were both wearing speedos, and it was enough to arouse the other four men.

"These are the speedos we took on cur orientation trip when we first joined the company," Tuck said. Brian added: "and they still fit."

Jeff and Jim looked at each other knowingly.

"What am I missing?" Ron asked.

"Maybe someday we'll let you in on a family secret," Jeff answered.

"No, now," Tucker said. "Brian and I have been talking, and we have an emotional need to share our love with our trusted and dear gay friends. We sort of want to come out, to be a part of the gay community. We know it's dangerous, but it's a need we have to fulfill."

Ron put his hand on Tuck's shoulder and said, "It's OK man. We suspected." That set everyone to laughing. "You two are so obviously in love."

Over breakfast, Brian and Tucker repeated the tale of how they met and fell in love at absolutely the wrong time. Ron interjected that there was never a wrong time to fall in love. He then wanted to know how they had the guts to come out to Jeff, their own son.

"They didn't," Jeff explained. I caught them at it one day, but I never told them until I came out."

"Wow, that's quite a story," Foster said. "It's got me as hard as a rock." Then he picked up his coffee cup as if to make a toast, "Here's to you both. May your double life continue to go smoothly and may you always be as happy as you are now. Your secret is safe with us."

Brian didn't know quite what to say and he sat motionless, but Tuck got up, and gave both Ron and Foster a kiss on the cheek.

Breakfast was finished and they had all consumed too much coffee, so the bathroom was suddenly the busiest room in the house. While everyone was relieving themselves, Jeff gathered up two blankets and plenty of towels to take down to the lake shore. He looked at Ron and said, "You and Foster can leave your clothes in our bedroom. We're going skinny dipping, if you have no objection."

"None whatsoever," Foster answered for both of them, and high tailed it into the bedroom. Jim and Jeff followed them in and threw their boxers on the bed with Ron's and Foster's clothes.

Ron started to laugh. "This is a first," He noted. I get to see my accountants' packages before I even hire them, and I sure like what I see. You're hired." They all laughed.

When they got out of the bedroom, Brian and Tucker were stripped and waiting for them in the living room. Foster thought to himself that he was right. Brian's prick was the thickest he'd ever seen, and Tucker's just about the longest. All in all, there was plenty of eye candy around, and he was looking forward to a romp in the lake. Ron looked at him and smiled. He could just about read Foster's thoughts.

They ran to the lake like little pre-teen boys. Jeff spread one blanket and Jim spread the other, while the fathers and the guests high tailed it quickly into the cool, inviting lake waters. Jim and Jeff followed right behind. Immediately they were in the lake, Brian, Tuck, Jeff and Jim started splashing each other and playing grab ass. Ron and Foster stood aside. They were not certain what to do. Jim motioned them over and they quickly joined in the fun. The activity was not, however, limited to grabbing asses, and every one got a good feel of every one else's cocks.

Jim, Jeff, Brian and Tucker, were not ready to share their mutual love with the others, so play time was limited to splashing each other and copping lots of feels. In spite of the fact that there wasn't a limp prick in the crowd, nobody allowed themselves to be brought to orgasm. Their horse play might not be acceptable behavior to some folk, but it was OK with these six guys, and they had a ball (no pun intended.)

It took a while for these six healthy specimens to tire, but tire they did. They crept up to the shore and collapsed on the blankets. Each of the three sets of lovers curled up together with their hands on one another's cocks and their lips pressed together. There was no intermingling this time. That would have to wait until fathers and sons were alone together again.

Before long they all fell asleep as the ever rising sun warmed their drying bodies. None of them woke up until the sun started its descent. They woke one by one and sat up on the blankets. Their erections had deserted them. Tuck asked if anyone was hungry, and they all groaned. They had had a huge breakfast and they were all still stuffed.

"I wouldn't mind something cold to drink," Foster said.

"Done," said Brian and off he went to the cabin. In a very short while he returned carrying a tray containing a pitcher of well-iced lemonade, six plastic cold cups and napkins. They finished off the pitcher in short order, and then they all lay down on the blankets again side by side, but not holding anybody else's body parts, and began to chew the fat.

Jeff and Jim questioned Ron about his business, making mental notes on what he needed by way of a bookkeeping system. Jim said, "Don't call us on Tuesday. We'll call you. I'll secure the necessary accounting programs, load your computer and get you started. Jeff noted that Jim took the initiative and was pleased that he didn't defer to him because he was the boss. He remarked to himself that they were equal in bed and he wanted Jim to be equal in business. Brian and Tuck picked up on this also and it somehow pleased them.

Foster said that he was just now looking for office space, and couldn't yet afford legal and accounting services, but would welcome any advice they could give him. They assured him that they would help him get started and wouldn't mind carrying him until he got his first client.

Tuck asked Ron and Foster, "Will you have time for an early dinner before you leave?"

Ron answered that they would, but his folks were making a farewell dinner. They did this every Sunday before the boys left, even though they knew they would be back the following Friday. Now that they were both self employed, they both took Fridays off, at least for the summer months, so they could have an extra long weekend in the country.

Ron noted that the sun was quite low in the sky and thought that they should be going. Nobody had thought to bring a watch with them, so they packed up and went back to the cabin. It was 3:30 PM. They all needed to pee but had to wait in line. While the others were taking their leaks, Ron had called his parents, and they extended an invitation for dinner to his new friends and accountants.

The invitation was accepted with pleasure. Ron told them that his folks lived in a white wooden frame house about fifty yards behind the store. The driveway runs along the right side of the store and he assured them that they couldn't miss it. He asked that they be there by 5:00 because they wanted to leave for the city by 6:30. Since nobody had eaten lunch, the early dinner hour was fine with all of them.

Even though the shower was barely big enough for one husky guy, Brian and Tuck showered together and then Jim and Jeff did the same. It's a mystery how they managed it, but they each got each other off before they completed their showers.

The Fishers greeted them warmly. They thanked them for being so kind to their son and Foster. It was obvious after a few minutes that they truly loved Foster as a son. Josie Fisher had made a delicious meat loaf which she served with mashed potatoes, peas, and homemade rolls. There was no beer on the table but Jason Fisher served them all red wine. Of course, the Fishers recognized Brian and Tucker from prior trips, and told them that it was a pleasure to finally meet them socially.

Everyone had a good laugh about the coincidence of Michael being a mutual friend and recommending Jeff and Jim to Ron for accounting services. 'Small world,' was a phrase heard several times around the dinner table. All good things have to come to an end, and Ron and Foster reluctantly said that they had to leave. There was much hugging and kissing along with promises to call each other Tuesday in the city.

The men offered the Fishers help in cleaning up, but they would have none of it. They stayed a while longer just to be polite and then they left also, thinking of the pleasures waiting for them at the cabin.

As soon as they reached the privacy of the cabin, they all stripped, and went out on the porch to enjoy the evening sunset. Jeff brought four beers out and they sat quietly for a while enjoying nature while they themselves were dressed in all of nature's glory.

Brian and Tucker were seated on the love seat. Jeff was in the chair next to his father and Jim was sitting in the chair next to Brian. Jeff leaned over and placed his hand on Tuck's thigh. Tuck's body shivered as Jeff's hand moved up toward his cock. Jeff wasn't even aware of what he was doing. It was an automatic reaction. His hand finally engulfed Tuck's rock hard erection and he began to stroke it gently. Tuck was breathless and moaned softly.

Brian and Jim became aware of what was going on. They smiled at each other and both reached over and took hold of the other's cock. They closed their eyes as their heads fell back and they started mewling with little sounds of pleasure.

"Sit on my lap son," Tuck said gently. As Jeff stood up to oblige his father, Tuck was busy spitting on his cock and lubricating it. Jeff knew exactly what to do. He straddled his dad and positioned Tuck's cock at the opening of his love canal. Tuck entered slowly, breathing hard and groaning softly. When he was all the way in, he stopped. There was no movement as father and son enjoyed the moment. Their lips met in a tender, loving kiss. The tips of their tongues caressed each other. Finally Jeff began to move up and down, and side to side. Tuck wanted to scream out and he did, "I love you Jeff. I love you. I love you."

Every time, Tuck felt himself cumming, he stopped Jeff's movements. Unfortunately Jeff was not so adept at prolonging his orgasm. He felt it coming on and he could not control it. With what can almost be called a howl, he let loose. His spunk spurted upwards toward his chest and toward Tuck's face. When he did that, his ass hole contracted and Tuck could no longer contain his orgasm either. He filled Jeff with several streams of his juices. The two collapsed in one another's arms with Tuck's cock up Jeff's ass until it fell out by a simple act of nature.

So what was happening to Brian and Jim? Just what you thought. Brian wanted Jeff and Tuck to be alone, so Brian, always thoughtful, took

Jim's hand. He led Jim into his bedroom. On the bed stand was a tube of lube. He told Jim to lie on his back. With much love and tenderness, he lubed Jim's ass and then he lubed his cock. He positioned himself between Jim's legs and slowly entered his newly adopted son. He pumped slowly and gently for a very long time. Jim rose to meet the rhythm, but like Jeff, he could not control himself and came in a loud scream of pleasure, causing Brian to shoot a load also.

They lay still for a very long while, kissing, hugging, and just cuddling. Finally they went to the bathroom to clean up, only to find Jeff and Tuck squeezed in the shower, kissing like crazy. They pounded on the shower door and Jim said, "Give us a chance to clean up also, would you?"

With their passions spent, Jeff and Jim went to bed together and Brian and Tuck went into their room also. They didn't bother to close their doors, but there were no further noises this night as both couples drifted off to sleep like babies.

The next day, their last day at the cabin, they didn't even bother to go skinny dipping. They made love in the cabin the entire day. They spent about an hour at a time with a different partner. Tuck was particularly aroused when he was with Jim because he kept thinking that Jim was fucking his little boy. The thought of it made him very horny.

At the same time, Jeff had the same horny experience with Brian. He kept thinking of the time when he was fifteen and he saw Tuck fucking this adorable, sweet, loving man.

As for Jim, I can't even describe how turned on he was when he was with Tuck or Brian. They were, after all, his partner's fathers. What a turn on.

Eventually they all separated, showered alone, and began to pack. After they loaded the van, they stripped the bed linen, and made sure the cabin was cleaned and neatened. They left the key under the mat. The landlord would send someone the next day to make the cabin ready for the next visitor.

As they started to get in to the car, Tuck looked back at the cabin and whined, "I'm sure going to miss this place."

"Amen," they all answered sadly.

CHAPTER TEN

Once back in the city, they all felt like they had never been away. Brian and Tuck avoided sex with their wives that Monday night, blaming exhaustion and the late hour. It was really true.

They went to the gym early Tuesday morning. There were more people there than usual. The fathers had no opportunity for even a quickie, but they were pretty sated anyway. Brian drove them to work feeling sorry for Tuck who had done the driving all weekend.

Unless they were certain that both of them would be in the office all day, Jim and Jeff took separate cars to work every morning. Often a client would call with a problem and they would have to run out to see the client and then come directly home from there. Tuesday morning they did their run as usual, showered, avoided hanky panky so they wouldn't be late to work, and took separate cars to work. They met at Denny's for breakfast. Then Jeff went to work and Jim stopped at a nearby Best Buy and bought Ron a good accounting program designed for professional businesses.

When he got to the office, Jeff told Jim that he had called Michael and set up a dinner date with him and Jerry for Thursday evening. He had then called Ron and cleared it with him and Foster, who would 'accidentally' run into them at the restaurant. "I also told him you'd be calling to come over and

71

set up his accounting system on his computer, and discuss the mundane fee situation. He cautioned us to go easy," Jeff laughed. "I assured him that we would make him an offer he couldn't refuse."

Jim hung up his jacket in his office and buzzed Jeannine. She was there in an instant with her steno pad. "You won't need that," he said. "Here's a new client's business card. Would you put the data in our computer system, and I'll give you his federal ID number after my first visit. Please call him for me and set up an appointment for us for today, if possible." As she started to leave, he added, "Thanks, Jeannine." With that she turned and smiled at him.

A few minutes later, she buzzed him and said that Ron Fisher was on the phone and would like to talk to him.

"Hi buddy," Ron's cheery voice greeted him. "How about we have lunch together, and we can work on the systems after lunch. Foster is available for lunch so would you see if Jeff can make it too."

"It's a go if we can find a place to eat where it's a certainty that Mike, I mean Michael, won't run into us," Jim answered. "I want him to be really surprised Thursday evening. By the way, Jerry will be there too, so I guess they are still going strong."

"No sweat." Ron said. "I just called his office. I needed to speak to him about a new problem, and his secretary told me that he had just left for a luncheon and seminar and it was at least an hour's drive away. I'll need to discuss that little problem with you also, so it will be a working lunch." That being said, Jim told Ron how to find the little restaurant that he and Jeff often ate lunch at and they agreed to meet at 12:30.

When the four guys met, the greeting was restricted to handshakes. They were all wearing suits, ties, the whole scene. For the entire world to judge, it was a typical business man's lunch. Once everyone's order was taken, Jim asked Ron, "So what's the big problem?"

"It's not really a problem. It's just a slight change in plans. Foster and I have been talking, and although a financial advisory office and an architectural office are not exactly compatible, we've decided to share office space until we both get going. It will sure save a lot of overhead," Ron explained.

"It sure will," Jeff agreed. "It's not as way out as you think. Have you ever heard of executive offices?" He didn't wait for an answer. "That's where a number of businesses lease one space, but each has a separate office and they each share one secretary. It's a real money saver, Economics 101," he concluded.

Jim added, "You can even share the accounting program I bought you. It can be set up for several different companies. I'll show you when we get to your office. Now let's talk about Thursday."

That got everyone laughing. They giggled like school girls plotting their big surprise for Michael.

Michael had chosen a gay owned restaurant that was not a strictly gay place. Although the vast majority of the patrons were gay, many straights frequented the restaurant as well. The food and service had received high praise by the food critic of the local newspaper and that had attracted a wide variety of diners.

Jim and Jeff were to meet Michael and Jerry there at 6:30 and Ron and Foster would come by at 6:45. This was their plan and this is what happened.

The restaurant was good at honoring reservations and the first arrivals were seated by 6:35. They ordered drinks but declined to order food just yet. While waiting for the drinks, Jim, who was sitting next to Jerry, put his hand on Jerry's arm, rubbed it seductively, and whispered, "So what's going on with you two?"

Before Jerry could answer, Jeff saw the second platoon enter the restaurant and he shouted to Jim, "Look who's here." Jim looked, and the two of them jumped up, ran to Ron and Foster, and the four got tangled up in hugs and what could only be described as passionate kisses.

Jerry didn't know who these guys were so he just looked curious, but Michael's jaw dropped. He sat glued to his chair. He saw Jeff approach the maitre'd. Some words were exchanged and their waiter approached their table. He told Michael and Jerry that they were moving them to a table for six.

There was a little confusion but eventually they were all seated. Michael found his voice, and he introduced Jerry to Ron and Foster. Then Jeff asked Michael, "You guys know each other?"

"Ron's my client and he was supposed to call you for accounting services."

"No kidding, "Jeff said.

"I just never got around to it, "Ron told the truth. "And when we met, I never connected the name. I didn't even look at the card you gave me," Ron advised Michael.

"So then how do you all know each other?" Michael wanted to know, more like he demanded to know.

By agreement Ron answered. He lowered his voice to a whisper so that he could not be heard beyond their table. "We met last weekend. We were all on a fishing trip. It was quite a weekend. We hit it off real well, and the four of us spent two days fucking and sucking. I can't remember how many times I changed partners. Can you remember Foster, honey? God my ass is still so sore, I can hardly take a dump. I'm just forced to hold it in."

Michael was speechless. After a little while, he managed to croak out, "What about your fathers, Jeff? Weren't they on the trip?"

"Oh they didn't mind a bit. My dad said that if it made Jim and me happy then he was happy for us."

Michael had been fooled up to now, but that last statement did not have a ring of truth.

"You guys are shitting me, aren't you?" he ventured, and they all broke out laughing. Then Jeff told him how they really met, but left out the skinny dipping and any other shenanigans.

Jeff continued, "Imagine how shocked we were when we put the pieces together and Ron discovered that I was the accountant he was supposed to call."

Michael interjected, "I'm kind of disappointed, Ron. I've been trying to get Jeff into bed with me for almost nine years and you raised my hopes with your horny tale, but it's all gone now." He put the back of his hand on his forehead in mock dismay.

"And what about how I feel?" Jerry asked. I had the hots for Jim all through college, and finally abandoned the cause. Listening to the story, I also thought that maybe my fantasies would come true. Alas it is not to be." Every body laughed, but Jim knew that Jerry really meant it.

"OK," Ron said looking at Michael. "We've worn this joke thin. I want to hear about you and Jerry."

Michael smiled at Jerry and put his hand on his. "There's not much to tell. When these two dyed in the wool straight men came out to me, I took them to a gay bar to celebrate. Jim's college room mate, and gay guy extraordinaire, was in the bar. He spotted Jim and ran over to find out what mister straight laced was doing there. Needless to say, he was as shocked as I was." Again he smiled at Jerry. "All I can tell you is that when I shook Jerry's hand a fire went through me. My whole body was charged. I wanted us to be together so badly, my guts hurt.

"Jeff and Jim had walked to work and I had driven them to the bar. Jerry had mentioned that he had come by cab, so when it came time to drive Jim and Jeff home, I asked Jerry if I could drive him home as well. Thank God, he accepted. After we dropped the Bobbsey twins off, I asked Jerry, no make that, begged Jerry, to come home with me. Miraculously he said he wanted to.

"We had sex that night, but it was like nothing I ever experienced before. I had an awakening that night. The love making was beyond belief because it was just that, love making, not just sex. I realized that I loved Jerry. I loved him enough to stop whoring around and to ask him to be my partner. The night was full of miracles. He agreed and told me that he felt the same way."

Everyone at the table had tears in their eyes. Jerry was sobbing outright. He had never been happier in his life, and listening to Michael tell everybody how much he loved him made Jerry even happier.

The crew was so joyous, and so comfortable with each other. They were bonding into a family unit, but didn't quite realize it at that moment in time. The restaurant could have served them shit and they would have thought it was the best gourmet meal they had ever eaten. But as a matter of fact, their meal was wonderful. They all ordered steak of different varieties. Each steak was cooked to perfection according to the diner's order. They talked long into the night until the waiter delicately informed them that the restaurant was closing.

They apologized profusely and reluctantly took their leaves.

As for Brian and Tucker, they continued to use the hourly hotel when they took a long lunch hour, but on sport nights, they went to their sons' apartment. They had their own key. When the sons were home they all played together, and if the boys were out, they played alone, keeping an eye on the clock.

Although they shared themselves often enough with their partners, Tuck and Jeff could not get enough of making love to each other, and when the foursome was together, the love making was heavily skewed in favor of Tuck and Jeff.

CHAPTER ELEVEN

Very early one Saturday morning in late September, when the fishing season was almost over, Jeff got a call from Ron who was in Lake Henry helping at his dad's store. Jeff was still half asleep and Jim was lying all over him. He had to push Jim over to reach the telephone.

"Hey Jeff, Ron. Did I wake you?"

Jeff mumbled into the phone, "Yes."

"Sorry," Ron said very unconvincingly. "Listen, you know that cabin your dads rented early in June? Well, it's for sale. The owner needs cash quick. He's really strapped. He's willing to let it go for way under market value. Would you, and maybe your fathers, be interested? Why don't you guys take a drive out today?"

"Hold on." Jeff nudged Jim awake, and he heard some unusual profanity coming from Jim. He quickly explained what was going on, and Jim seemed interested.

"I'm not sure about buying the place," Jim said, "but I wouldn't mind driving out for the weekend. Tell Ron we'll be there by noon."

They got to the store just before noon. Ron had arranged for his dad to cover for him, and he had made an appointment to meet the realtor at the cabin at 1 PM.

The four young men grabbed some junk food from the store for lunch, climbed into Jeff's car and headed for the cabin. In the car, Jeff said, "Guys, Jim and I were talking on the way up. What if the four of us, Michael and Jerry bought the place together? We'd always have a weekend get away, together or separately. We could even heat the place for winter use."

"Not a bad idea," Foster said but we'd need at least one more bedroom."

"I know," Jeff answered. "You're our resident architect. When we get there, tell us if it would be feasible to add two bedrooms, a bath and a heating system. If the price is as good as you say it is, it might be worth it to do an expansion. If we need extra money, I'm sure we could get a mortgage."

"Wow, this is a lot to digest," Ron said. "Let's see what happens."

They found the key to the cabin under the welcome mat, where it was the first time they arrived there, and where they had left it. Since they were all familiar with the cabin, Foster got busy immediately doing his thing. He walked all around the house and even looked into the crawl space underneath the house. When the realtor arrived, he had nothing to do but stand around. He was a good looking man in his late thirties who kept ogling all four men and trying very hard not to look at their packages. He was losing the battle. All he could hope for was that they would be the ones to buy the place. Hell, he wouldn't even mind giving up his commission. Lust is a terrible monster.

Foster came in and sat down. He asked the realtor, Dan Harriman, if he had some paper and a pen he could borrow. Dan had a legal pad with him and he handed it to Foster along with a pen. Quickly, Foster made a rough sketch of the existing building. Then he drew a wing extending from the dining room.

"Look," he said. "If we remove the sliding glass doors in the dining room and put in a standard door we could build a hallway going out toward the lake. There's room for two bedrooms on the right side of the hallway with a bathroom between them. We could put a laundry room with a furnace behind the bathroom, and it would be easy to bring in vents and heat the place. We'd have to enter the laundry/furnace room through the bathroom, but hell, it's only a summer cabin after all." Then he added, "See, now the structure becomes L shaped. We could put a big sundeck in the L and still have a beautiful view of the lake."

To a man they could picture themselves in the nude, sunbathing on the deck, and their excitement over buying the place really took hold of them.

"I've gotta call Michael," Jeff said. He excused himself and went outside for privacy. He knew that if he used a bedroom they would hear every word. He pulled out his cell phone and was happy that Michael picked up on the first ring.

"Is Jerry there? Good." He took his time and explained about Ron's early morning call, the drive out to the country, Foster's expansion proposal, and his idea that the six of them buy it together for a weekend and vacation getaway home. Michael said that he would call right back. He explained what was going on to Jerry, who became very enthusiastic. Jerry was in commercial real estate, but wanted to be there, because he was certain he could then negotiate the realtor's fee. Little did he know the realtor was ready to drop his commission all together for these hunks.

Michael called Jeff back. "Give me directions to the place. We can get there by 4 PM. Jerry says to offer the realtor a refundable check as earnest money, and ask him if we can use the cabin tonight. We'll have no place else to stay." Jeff gave him directions to the store and said that they would meet them there. "We're on our way," Michael said.

Jeff told Dan that one of the prospective buyers was a commercial real estate broker. He offered what Jerry had suggested and was surprised at how accommodating Dan was. He also asked that they wait on negotiating the selling price until the other two got here. Jeff gave Dan a $50 check and they arranged to meet back at the cabin at 4:30. Dan gave them his card in case they needed to call him or had more questions. He left them there in the cabin and said he'd see them later.

When he was gone, Ron said, "I can't tell you all how exciting this is." He grabbed both Jeff and Jim, pulled them to him and kissed them both. Foster joined them in a group hug. Just like that they all had boners.

Jeff had to pull away or something might happen that shouldn't. He changed the subject by asking Foster "Is there anything we can do about sound proofing this place? You can hear every creak in the beds from anywhere in the house."

"Not a big problem. We can blow insulation into the walls. It will muffle sound and help keep the place warm in winter."

"That's a relief," Jim said. "I don't relish the thought of hearing you guys and Michael and Jerry making love noises all night."

"We better get back to the store and wait for the terrible twosome." Ron suggested.

When they returned, they found both Mom and Pop Fisher in the store. It was pretty busy so Ron and Foster chipped in to help. When things got quieter, Ron filled his parents in and what was happening. They got so excited at the thought that Ron, Foster and his friends would be spending weekends out here, even in the winter, that they didn't even mind that Ron and Foster would be sleeping at the cabin instead of at their house.

The store had a front porch with several wing back chairs. The late September day was unusually warm so Jim and Jeff sat outside waiting for their friends and old college room mates. They arrived about 3:45 PM ahead of schedule. They all went into the store and Ron introduced them to his folks.

Josie Fisher said she wanted them all to have dinner at her house that evening, but Ron said that was not an option. Tonight they were all going out to dinner to celebrate. He was assuming that their real estate deal would go through. He called Joey's Place, the barbeque restaurant they had all enjoyed so much on Jim and Jeff's last visit, and made reservations for eight at 7:00 PM.

The young real estate entrepreneurs then headed off to the cabin. They managed to get by with one car by Jerry sitting in Michael's lap. Michael didn't seem to mind at all. Jeff showed the newcomers around the place and Foster showed them his sketch. Michael asked Foster how much he thought the expansion would cost. He reckoned about $17,000. Jim said immediately, "That's only a little over $2,800 split 6 ways."

"The seller wants only $35,000 for the cabin and the 4 acres of land it sits on," Ron said, "but I'm pretty sure he'll take $30,000. That's only $5,000 each. It's less than $8,000 total for each of us if we pay all cash, but between an investment advisor, accountants, a commercial real estate agent and a lawyer, we all have good banking contacts. Getting a mortgage shouldn't be a problem. Conservatively speaking, if we add another $5,000 for new furniture, we're talking about a total cost of $52,000. If we put 20% down, that's $10,400 or roughly $1,700 each for the down payment, and we can easily mortgage the rest. We can set up a joint bank account for the running of this place. I'm really excited and I'm voting yes," he said.

Michael yelled out, "All those in favor say, aye."

"Aye," they all yelled together.

Just at that moment Dan arrived. Ron introduced him to Michael and Jerry, and added the extra information that Michael had been Jeff's room mate in college and Jerry had been Jim's. Dan shook both their hands and got hornier than ever. He had never seen a more handsome crew.

Jerry took over. He offered $30,000. He knew it was $5,000 less than the seller wanted, but if Dan was willing to cut his commission from 6% to 4%, the deal would be sweetened and the seller might find it more acceptable.

Dan replied, "Well let's see." He took out his cell phone and called his client in Los Angeles. His children had made him move out there because he was getting on in years, and they wanted him nearby so they could look after him.

Dan went outside, both for privacy and for better cell phone reception. Inside the cabin, they could still hear bits and pieces of the conversation. Dan was smiling so they were encouraged. When he came inside, he reported, "Well it's a little less than he hoped to get since he feels he's giving the place away anyhow, but given the situation and his distance away, he's really glad to unload the place. He says yes, and wishes you all good health and good luck in your new cabin."

Then Dan asked, "How long will you all be here before you return to the city?"

"We can stay until early evening tomorrow," Michael replied for the crew.

"Good, I'll get all the papers ready for your signatures by early afternoon tomorrow. Monday morning, I'll overnight the signed papers to LA and ask them to sign them and overnight them back. I'll need at least a $1,000 deposit guys. Shall I bring them here or to your parents' home, Ron?" he asked.

"Bring them here," several voices answered at once, and someone added, "You're welcome to join us skinny dipping. None of us packed anything, certainly not Speedos." Dan's crotch swelled.

He asked, "Will it be alright if I bring my partner. Since we are going to be neighbors, I'd like him to meet you guys."

Michael put an arm around Dan's shoulder, and lamented, "Man, what's happened to my gaydar. I never suspected." He lied.

Dan shook each one's hand and left. Jim, always the thoughtful one, turned on the circuit breaker. The boys locked up their cabin and hid the key. They went back to the Fishers in preparation for dinner at Joey's Place.

In the car back, Foster said, "I'm going to ask Dan to recommend a couple of good contractors and I'll contact them during the week. I'll get blueprints ready for them to bid on. Who wants to handle the mortgage application, lawyer, accountant or financial analyst?"

Jeff said, "I've brought several clients to my bank recently for loans and mortgages. I've got good contacts there so let me handle that. I'll get on it first thing Monday."

It seems they all wanted to get things moving at once.

When they came back to the Fishers, they washed up. They couldn't change clothes because nobody had thought to bring a change, but they all knew that they wouldn't need any tomorrow anyhow.

Ron drove Foster, Michael and Jerry to the restaurant, and the Fishers drove Jim and Jeff. As the two cars parked in the parking lot, a third car pulled in to the space next to Ron's and out came Dan and a very handsome gentleman about the same age as Jeff's fathers, very early fifties. He was, tall, lean, muscular and a total knockout. Dan greeted every body warmly, and made all the introductions. Warren, Dan's partner, just happened to be the town sheriff.

Ron asked if they would like to join them in celebrating their purchase. It seemed appropriate to everyone that he and Warren should join them. They accepted and were more than happy to be in the company of such good looking guys. Ron also reminded them of the skinny dipping party for men only at the cabin the next afternoon.

The food, service and hospitality at Joey's Place were as good as Jim and Jeff remembered. The good cheer and laughter coming from their table ignited joy throughout the entire restaurant. Nobody sent over free drinks this time but Joey himself provided two pitchers of free beer. It seems everyone already knew that the Fisher boy had purchased the cabin with some of his friends, and Joey wanted to welcome the city boys as part time neighbors. It occurred to Jeff that this would be a gay tolerant, if not gay friendly, place to live. They even had a gay sheriff.

By the end of the evening, Dan and Warren did not just say goodbye, they hugged everyone warmly before departing. When the crew got back to the Fishers, Ron raided the shelves for provisions for breakfast and lunch the next day. He also threw in some toiletries because nobody had expected to stay over night. He put a couple of sleeping bags in the trunk of his car, and put the food on the back seat. Reluctantly he told his folks that it wouldn't be convenient for everyone to make church tomorrow as they did not have proper clothing with them. He promised that they would be better prepared in the future. His folks said that they certainly understood. He and Foster went to the cabin in his car. The others each took their own cars to the cabin.

When they arrived, they all helped Ron unload the car and put the food in the fridge. Unknown to everyone Ron had put a bottle of champagne in with the provisions. Now he popped the cork while Jeff took out juice glasses. "We gotta buy some wine glasses," Jeff said to no one in particular.

It was a spectacular night so they took two kitchen chairs out on the porch to make room for all of them. There they toasted themselves and their new acquisition. They sat on the porch for a long time, sipping champagne and chewing the fat until Jeff finally said, "Hey guys I'm tired," and that put a period to the evening.

Michael and Jerry took what had been Brian's and Tucker's bedroom. Out of habit Jim and Jeff took the other one. Ron and Foster said that the night was too good to waste and they were going to sleep on the porch. Ron went inside and brought out the two sleeping bags. "Do you think we could both squeeze into one of those things?" Foster asked.

We can only presume that they all intended to go to sleep.

CHAPTER TWELVE

Jim and Jeff undressed to the buff and climbed into bed. It had been a long and exciting day, and neither had thought much about getting their rocks off. They just lay there, all wrapped up in each other, kissing and fondling. If they fell asleep, fine, and if they proceeded to full blown passionate sex that would be fine too.

Suddenly Jeff started to giggle.

"What's so funny?" Jim wanted to know

"I was just thinking of the sounds my dads made the last time we were here. Hell we are really very quiet compared to them. They could be heard in China. And speaking of that, it's awfully quiet next door. Do you think they really went to sleep?" Jeff wondered aloud.

"For sure I know that Jerry is a noisy cummer. Maybe they're more tired than we are," Jim said. The words were no sooner out of his mouth when they could hear the moaning from next door. The sound of a creaking bed was hardly noticeable at first, but in time it got louder and more insistent. Now there was a steady rhythm of creaking bed springs and the moaning of bodies in ecstasy.

They lay quietly for a while. The sex in the next room had not yet made them horny enough to get going in earnest. Then Jim asked very wistfully,

"Do you hear that low moan under the shriller one? That's Jerry. I told you that in college we whacked off together almost every night. He was in his bed and I was in mine, of course. I'd lay there stroking my boner, listening to his moans, and think of the time I caught Michael and my brother doing it to each other. I never could get up the courage to ask Jerry if he wanted to do me and I'd do him. When we graduated he told me that I was the object of his masturbation fantasies. He wanted us to do it mutually so badly that he hurt. He said the hardest thing he ever did in his life was not to come on to me in four years of sharing a room."

Jeff thought a moment and then he said, "Funny, Michael and I never jerked off together in our dorm room, but we talked about our sex lives all the time. He would make a joke of it, but I knew he meant it when he said he dreamed that I would switch teams and he could then be my catcher. Now I realize that when he said 'dreamed,' he too was letting me know that I was his masturbation fantasy."

They became very silent, listening to the noises getting louder next door. After a while Jim said to Jeff, "Sweetheart, do you remember how it was when your fantasy came true with your two dads? You told me that it heightened your sex with me and that sex with your dads was absolutely incredible. Your love making to me was more intense than it had ever been. I know that you fantasize you're with Brian and Tucker when you make love to me, and I don't care. I know it's me you want and love, and your fantasies, especially the fulfilled fantasies, have made you into a fucking sex machine. I'm not complaining at all, just commenting."

They became silent again until Jeff whispered to Jim, "Are you saying that if we allowed Michael's and Jerry's masturbation fantasies to come true, we would be increasing their sexual pleasure and probably ours?"

"I'm only saying that it seems that the more fantasies we have while making love, especially when they are fulfilled, the more pleasure we seem to get out of sex," Jim tried to explain.

Jeff was silent for a moment. The groaning next door was reaching a fever pitch. He jumped out of bed.

"Where are you going?" Jim asked.

"I'm going to have Michael tonight and I'll send Jim right in to you. I've got to do it quickly before I chicken out." He was gone in a flash.

He was very surprised to find Michael's and Jerry's door wide open. He could clearly see them in the moonlight that was streaming into the room. Michael was lying on top of Jerry. Jerry's legs were wrapped around Michael's waist. They were kissing madly as Michael was pumping hard in Jerry's bum hole.

"Stop," Jeff yelled a little too loudly.

Michael had never fallen out of an ass hole so fast and he fell to the floor yelling, "What the fuck! You scared the shit out of me. Is the place on fire or something?"

"What's wrong?" Jerry cried.

"Nothing is wrong. Just listen to me," Jeff implored them. "I don't want to get into the details right now, but I've had a masturbation fantasy since I was fifteen years old."

"So what's so unusual about that?" Michael demanded to know.

"I know that's not unusual. What's unusual is that recently my fantasy came true, and after it did, my sex life with Jim, which was fantastic, improved to extraordinary. My fantasy lover reports the same thing happened for him and his partner."

Michael said very matter of factly, "You mean you finally had sex with your dad, or was it both of them?"

Michael was dumbfounded. "How in the world...?"

"My God, Jeff. Don't you see how they look at each other? And you look at them in the same way. I guess I've suspected since the night I met them in our dorm room. And what pray tell is the fantasy or fantasies you are proposing for Jerry and me?"

"Well, you always told me that you dreamed I'd switch teams, and Jerry, you always told Jim that you wished that you two had masturbated each other during all those college years and how hard it was for you to keep your distance all that time. So Jim and I want you to fulfill your fantasies." He looked at Jerry. "Jim is waiting for you."

"I guarantee from experience, the four of us will love each other more," he added.

"What do you think?" Jerry asked Michael even though he already knew the answer.

"Jerry, Jeff said that Jim is waiting for you," Michael said to Jerry. That being said, he grabbed Jeff around his neck and pulled him in to a very wet and sexy kiss, simultaneously grinding his very hard prick into Jeff's very eager one.

Jerry ran out of the room and bumped into Jim.

"I was wondering what was going on. It was taking so lo..." Jim couldn't finish the sentence because Jerry's lips on his prevented it.

When the two sets of pinch hitters were in separate beds, Jeff and Jim asked the same question of their new lovers. "What was it exactly that you fantasized so I can make it all come true?"

For the next three hours the two couples, sucked, fucked and rimmed continuously. They would bring themselves close to climax and stop. They were all expert at prolonging orgasm as long as possible. But all good things come to an end. In the wee hours of the morning they finally were fully spent, and fell asleep in one another's arms. Just as he was falling asleep, Michael asked Jeff, "Do you think Jim and I could have a go at it, and you and Jerry?"

"I don't see why not," was Jeff's answer.

In the morning all four of the friends were sound asleep when Ron and Foster came in the house to relieve themselves. Both bedroom doors were wide open and they could see immediately that the configuration of bodies was out of sync.

It had never been Jeff's nor Jim's intention to ignore Ron and Foster, but they had never shared the fantasies that the other four had. It just had never occurred to them to include their other best friends. When Ron and Foster saw that the other four had obviously had sex together, they were mildly upset.

"Look at them?" Ron said to Foster. "They had a party after we went to sleep and we weren't included. This partnership is off to a bad start," he said rather sarcastically. They went into the bathroom to pee, and afterward Ron jumped into bed with Michael and Jeff, and Foster jumped into bed with Jim and Jerry.

Before the sleeping beauties knew what was happening Ron was sucking Michael's dick and stroking Jeff's. In the other bed, Foster was sucking Jim's cock and stroking Jerry's.

"Wait," Jim yelled and he and Jerry jumped out of bed and headed for the bathroom with Michael and Jeff in close pursuit. When everybody's nature calls were answered, the two threesomes resumed where they had left off, and another fantastic round of lovemaking ensued.

It was almost eleven, when the party finally broke up and everyone realized that they were really hungry.

"Also," Ron reminded everyone, "Dan and Warren are joining us for an afternoon of skinny dipping."

They washed up, and satisfied their hunger pangs with coffee and a toasted bagel for breakfast. Nobody bothered to dress because they hadn't brought swim suits and they were hosting a nude bathing party that afternoon anyway. Strangely none of them mentioned the sexual activity of yesterday night and of this morning. They didn't have to. There was so much love in that cabin, that there was no room for doubts or regrets. Each couple loved each other, and nothing was going to change that, but as a group, they loved each other like a band of brothers. They all felt it instinctively, and each time one or another would pass close to someone else, they would grab each other in a bear hug. Jeff was convinced that he had been correct in allowing Michael and Jerry to live out their fantasies. Ron and Foster were an added bonus to what he thought of as their crew. A bond had been formed here that would last a life time.

After breakfast, they cleaned up the kitchen and brought two blankets and several towels down to the lake shore. The late September sun was unusually warm, but not much of a burn threat. Needless to say, young as they were, they were still exhausted. As soon as each one lay down on the blanket with his partner, he fell asleep.

They were awakened by the sound of a horn blasting. Dan and Warren had arrived. They had foreseen that there would be little or no provisions at the cabin so they had packed several picnic baskets which were on the back seat and bags full of goodies in the trunk. The guys all ran to greet them and to help unload the car. It didn't seem a problem that they were all naked. Dan and Warren were wearing shorts and sandals and nothing else, not even underwear. When the perishables were refrigerated, Dan and Warren shed their shorts and went down to the lake. By now, the crew was refreshed from their nap and they all went right into the water.

It started with the usual splashing and laughing, but quickly progressed to cock and ass grabbing. The crew had no problem with it, but to their credit, it didn't take Dan and Warren long to catch on to the rules of the game and to join in. Obviously every one of them was as hard as a rock.

Warren and Dan were not as sex weary as the others. They had been stroking each other, as well as some other strange cocks, under the water, and they could not control them selves. They supported one another in the water to keep from sinking as they came almost simultaneously. Both of them turned red, but the others all applauded, slapped them on the back, and gave them hugs to let them know it was OK with them all.

Eventually they all tired and retreated to the lure of the beach blankets. They sunbathed in the early autumn sun, but it began to get cooler as the day grew older, so they packed up and went into the cabin. They showered two at a time in very cramped corners just to rinse off the lake water. It killed them to do it, but they even dressed.

Dan and Warren had brought fried chicken, corn on the cob, potato chips, and paper napkins. Ron had brought soda and beer along with plastic cups, flatware and plates. It was too crowded around the table so they decided to eat buffet style. Jeff made a mental note to get a larger dining room table and more dining room chairs.

Jeff and Jim set out all the dishes, flatware, cups and napkins on the dining room table. Ron and Foster found some stack tables in the kitchen pantry and set them out. "Dig in," someone said, and they did.

They stuffed themselves and then sat around chewing the breeze and just plain enjoying each other's company. Finally Jeff said, "Since Jim, Ron, Foster and I set everything up, the rest of you can clean up. There used to be plastic garbage bags under the sink. Everything was disposable so just dump everything in a bag, clean the place up, and close it up until next weekend."

After the cleanup crew was done and everything was shipshape, Dan went out to his car and got the offering papers and a few other documents. Michael looked them all over, and the six partners signed where it was indicated. Dan returned Jeff's $50.00 check and Jeff gave him another for $1.000.00. Jeff and Jim were elected to keep an accounting and they would all adjust the investment later on. Then Foster asked Dan to recommend some contractors for the renovation. He gave Foster two names and their telephone numbers.

With the business out of the way, Dan and Warren left, but not without hugs and warm kisses from all. "See you guys next weekend," Warren said, "and drive within the speed limit. I'd hate to have to run you in or ticket you."

That was meant to get a laugh and it did.

They closed up the cabin, locked the door, and put the key under the mat. Each couple got into their own car and they caravanned back to the city. They all had the same thought. This was going to be a great place for the crew to get away weekends and vacations, and enjoy their brotherhood. They were all so very excited. How lucky they were and what a great family they were going to be.

Jeff wondered if the others would mind if his dads came out two or three weekends a year, after the addition was completed, of course. He doubted they would mind. All of them now knew his dads' story and were most sympathetic.

When they finally got into their apartment, Jeff and Jim took a proper shower and then hurried into bed. As they made love that night their heads danced with visions of fucking and being fucked by Brian and Tucker and the crew. Every member of the crew had the same thoughts invading their fantasies, and just as Jeff had promised, their sex that night was extraordinary.

CHAPTER THIRTEEN

The crew was too excited to do much work all during the next week. They managed to do what they had to do and delayed anything that they thought could be delayed.

On Monday Foster called both contractors and made an appointment with one of them for 9 AM on the following Saturday, and the other at 11 AM.

Jeff made an appointment with his banking contacts for 2 PM that afternoon and when he told Michael at lunch, Michael insisted on going with him. After he made the appointment with the bank, Jeff called his dad, Tucker. He told Tuck what was going on with the purchase and what plans they had for enlarging the facility. He also stressed that there would be four bedrooms and only three couples purchasing the property. He told Tuck that he was certain that nobody would mind if they used the place whenever they could, just as they used his and Jim's condo.

Tucker immediately called Brian's office and told him what was happening. Brian was excited for the boys, of course, but thinking about being able to use the cabin more often put a bulge in his pants so he asked Tuck if he wanted to take a longer than usual lunch hour today. Tucker could never say no to his beloved Brian.

At two o'clock promptly, Jeff and Michael arrived at the office of Roger Allen. Roger was the senior loan officer at the bank. Senior or not, Rog was only three years older than they. He was a handsome, athletic guy. You knew he was all man, in fact, a man's man, whatever that means. His wife had once represented their state in the Miss America contest. He had three strapping sons all destined to be MVP on some athletic team.

Rog knew that Michael was gay. When he first began to do business with him and Jeff, he was guarded, and definitely uncomfortable. Recently he learned that Jeff was gay also. Once he realized that they were not going to attack him and take his virgin ass, he began to relax. He also began to respect their business acumen and their honesty in being open about their sexual preference. He especially got a kick out of Michael and the jokes he made about his 'gayness.' In a short time he became gender blind, and never thought of them as anything but good business associates. They had certainly brought a lot of business his way.

Roger motioned for them to sit. "What's going on gentlemen?" he asked. To which funny guy Michael responded, "You don't know us well enough to call us gentlemen." Yuk, Yuk. Jeff told Michael to cool it and then he turned to Rog and told him about the cabin, it's peaceful seclusion, it's serenity, it's fishing, and on and on.

"You really like this place, I gather," Roger quipped.

"You might say that," Michael responded and laughed.

Jeff went on to explain that the cabin and four acres of forest were being purchased by six working professionals for $30,000. He told Roger about the proposed expansion, which the architect, one of the buyers, put at about $17,000. And finally he said they figured the new furniture and some replacement pieces would cost another $5,000 for a total of $52,000. They were going to put $10,400 down and wanted to mortgage the remaining $41,600 which all six were willing to obligate themselves to so there was little risk to the bank.

Roger listened intently and was actually jealous. He loved his wife and kids, but supporting them and seeing to their needs, did not include a country getaway. He also had visions of the six gay men in orgiastic coupling and he felt it in his groin. He roused himself from his reverie and asked for the address of the property. Then he took a small pamphlet from his desk and looked up the nearest branch office to the property. He called the loan officer at the branch and asked him to please get an appraisal on the land and structure as soon as possible. There was a long period of silence while Rog listened intently. He thanked his associate and hung up.

He turned to Jeff and Michael and told them that they could only be awarded a mortgage which was no more than ninety percent of the appraised value of the property, but with so many solid signatories, he could give them an unsecured loan for the balance.

"Now," he said to Jeff, "get out your pencil. "John, the loan officer at the branch out there, told me that he got a call from a realtor named Dan Harriman, a week ago. Dan told him that the property was going on the market and asked him for a bank appraisal which Dan paid for. Now hear this," he said dramatically. "John said that property values out there have been steadily rising, but in the last two years they have seen a tremendous boom out there caused by city folks buying land and putting up vacation homes. I'm glad you guys are sitting. The bank already has the appraisal on file. They have valued each of the four acres at $6,500 each, and they appraised the cabin, as is, at $41,000. Check me Jeff, but isn't that $67,000? Ninety percent of that is $60,300. I hereby approve your request for $41,600. In fact, why not make it an even $45,000 and get better furniture."

Jeff and Michael jumped up and clasped Roger's hand. They were beaming.

"OK, here's what I need. I want full name, address, date of birth and social security number of all six buyers. Give me the telephone number of the realtor. I'll need to know the bottom line on the closing statement so I can send him a bank check for the mortgage amount. I'll send another bank check, made out to all six of you for the balance of the $45,000. Who should I send that check to?"

Michael answered, "Send it to Jeff. He's officially handling the accounting and I'll make Jim audit him." Everybody laughed at that.

"I'll get all the property information I need from this Dan Harriman, and I'll have all the papers ready for signature tomorrow afternoon. Do you think you can muster the troops and get everyone up here for signing tomorrow at 4:30 PM?"

"That's not a problem," Jeff answered, "but we don't call ourselves the troops. We refer to ourselves as the crew."

"So be it," Rog answered. He stuck out his hand and said, "OK guys. I'll see you tomorrow."

The next day, they all converged on Roger's office and signed all the papers. Ron suggested that they celebrate by having dinner out this evening at a really good restaurant. They decided on a new French restaurant nearby that was receiving rave reviews by anyone they knew who had been there. Rog told them that he had taken his wife there on their anniversary, and they had enjoyed the place immensely. That sealed it.

Rog shook each of their hands as they left and wished them all well. Jeff told him that as soon as he got the check for the mortgage, he would deposit it in a new 'cabin account' at this bank. He thanked him also for his confidence in the crew, and for his exceptional speed handling their application.

The next morning, Dan called Michael and told him that he had received all the papers back from Los Angeles. He was aware that they had received a mortgage commitment because he had just spoken to Roger Allen, who told him he would express the check from the bank so that they could close that weekend when the crew was there. They set the closing in Dan's Office for Saturday at 4 PM. Michael made the late appointment so as not to interfere with Foster's interviews with the contractors. As soon as he got off the phone he called the others and told them they had to have checks with them for the closing on Saturday. The reaction was a universal whoopee.

This time when the crew packed for the weekend, they made sure they had appropriate clothing. They knew how important it was for the Fishers that they all attend church together on Sunday morning and they didn't want to disappoint. This weekend would also take them into October. The Fishers general store would close for the winter in two weeks.

During the past week the weather had changed drastically. Indian summer was over, and it was much colder. There would be no swimming this time and since there was no heat in the cabin, they also packed warmer clothing and warm sleeping bags. Ron and Foster had tipped them off that two guys in one sleeping bag was really cozy.

Nobody had a car that seated more than five persons so they decided to go up on Friday evening with two cars. Jim and Jeff split up. Jim drove with Michael and Jerry and Jeff with Ron and Foster. On the way up Jeff said that he was close to having to trade his car. It had a lot of miles on it from running from client to client. He told Ron and Foster that he would trade in for a seven seater mini van. This way they need only use one car going to the cabin and they could start to economize.

They stopped first at the Fishers who were expecting them. Of course Josie had a great meal ready for them for dinner. She made a healthy salad followed by not so healthy grilled pork chops with sweet potato fries. For desert she served apple cobbler with coffee.

When he had finished eating, Jeff stood up and wrapped his arms around Josie in a bear hug. He thanked her for all of them, and told her she couldn't do this every weekend because she would spoil them. "Anyway," he said, "when the addition is finished we'll make our own meals."

When they got up to leave, they all kissed Mom and Pop Fisher good night, and the Fishers told Ron not to rush in to the store the next morning. They weren't expecting much traffic in this weather.

At the cabin, they made a big ceremony of taking the key from under the mat and opening the door. They brought in the weekend gear they had taken with them plus the box of food that Ron had taken from the store.

"Michael said, "Look we've got to stop taking stuff from the store without paying. It's not fair to Ron's folks."

"I tried to pay them guys, but my dad said that he owed me much more for all the days I worked the store for him so that he could take a day off. I argued, but he wouldn't give in."

Michael said he had a surprise also. He went to his car, opened the trunk and took out a little space heater. It's not much he said but we can all huddle in the living room. They set the heater up and in time the living room was toasty. The refrigerator still held beer from the previous weekend and Ron had brought a couple of six packs. After they unpacked they all got cozy in the living room and opened a can of beer each. They sat silently for a pretty long time, and then Jeff said, "I love you guys. Thanks for being in my life."

Jim didn't want to show the guys that he had started to cry when Jeff said that, so he jumped on Jeff and started to wrestle with him. Bam, in a flash, the six of them were wrestling on the floor. The wrestling turned to kissing and fondling, and thank goodness the heater was doing its work, because little by little clothes were being shed. Bodies became entangled without regard to who belonged to whom. Laughing and giggling they formed into a daisy chain on the living room floor with the coffee table in the middle of the circle. They purposely made sure that the cock in their mouth was not their partner's. The noise stopped when they began sucking in earnest. They each came within a two minute period swallowing every drop they could, and keeping the living room floor perfectly clean.

They began to crawl around like male dancers in a modern ballet, until each of the partners was in the arms of his own partner. The partners cuddled and fondled themselves, but occasionally a hand would reach out and touch the couple lying next to them. They lay that way a long time until Jeff realized that Jim had fallen asleep in his arms, and he suggested that they turn in.

Ron and Foster said that the living room was too warm for the sleeping bags, but they would crash here and sleep on top of the bags. The others went to the rooms they had used last weekend. They didn't close the doors for two reasons. First, some of the warmth from the space heater filtered into the bedrooms, and second, they didn't need to. Each couple cuddled naked in one sleeping bag and that was warm enough.

Fortunately, they did not wake up at the same time or the bathroom could not have handled the traffic. One by one they did their morning things and washed up. It was too cold to shower. Ron made coffee and toast with butter and jam for breakfast. He told them that he knew of a nice little diner up the road where they could have lunch and of course he suggested Joey's for dinner. They all agreed.

After breakfast, they cleared the table and Foster spread out the blueprints for the addition that he had meticulously drawn up during the week. Promptly at nine the first contractor arrived. He was overweight and constantly puffed when he talked trying to inhale more air. But he was very business like. He and Foster reviewed the plans down to the last detail. When he was through he took out his estimating pad and worked up a detailed estimate of $18,200. Even though his huffing and puffing annoyed Foster, he was impressed with the man's professionalism. Before he left, Joe Torrance of Torrance Construction Company, gave each member of the crew his business card.

"Well, that's somewhat higher than I thought, but not too far out of line," Foster said, clearly disappointed. The men sat around gabbing while waiting for Randy Jones of Jones Construction to show up. They wished they had more time before his visit which was now only a half hour away. They all wanted to play games like last night, but they had to wait.

About 10:45 Randy knocked at the door. A contractor who was fifteen minutes early, really impressed Foster. His experience was that you were lucky if they bothered to show up at all. Six feet, five inches of Randy ducked through the door. He was built like a football line backer, and couldn't have been more than twenty years old. Foster was afraid he wouldn't have the right experience for the job, so before he even showed Randy the blueprints, he interrogated him about his background and credentials. It turned out that in spite of his youthful appearance, Randy was twenty seven. He had been working for his father all through his school years, since he was twelve. His dad recently retired and he had taken over the business. Foster was satisfied and he opened up the blueprints and spread them on the table.

He and Foster talked for almost two hours and Randy asked every imaginable question. He not only wanted to know about the physical structure, he wanted to know about the men who would be using it so he could custom build to their needs. Foster was more than impressed and prayed he would give them a good estimate. Finally, he took out his estimating pad, and a calculator. He began to gather the numbers and when he was through, the bottom line was $16,500.

"I do a lot of the work myself so I can keep the costs down," he explained.

Foster said, "We're closing this afternoon at 4 PM so how soon could you start and when can you finish?"

"It slows down this time of year, I could probably start by mid week and this place would be ready for your use for the Christmas holidays. Actually," he added, "I might even have it for Thanksgiving but I don't want to hang my hat on that."

Foster said, "All those in favor say aye." The ayes had it.

"Where's your closing at?" Randy wanted to know. "I can work up the contract and bring it to you there for signature and I'll need at least 10% to start the job. You can hold back 20% until we get the CO. I'll ask for progress payments as I go."

"Fair enough," Foster said.

"It's a deal," Jeff said. He figured that he would advance the check and get it covered Monday morning. "Do you know where Dan Harriman's office is? That's where we'll be at 4 PM."

"I'll be there." Randy answered.

"Hey Randy," Ron said. "We're going to Rosie's for lunch. Would you care to join us?"

"I sure would," he said. Then I gotta rush back to my office and get the contracts ready. I'll have it ready before you leave Dan's office." He said 'Dan' like he knew him well.

The crew had to take two cars and Randy drove his truck to Rosie's for a quick getaway. On the way over Foster called Joe Torrance and told him that they wouldn't need his services and thanked him for giving them his time.

After they ordered sandwiches and a drink, curious Michael asked Randy if he was married:

No!

Did he have a girl friend?

No!

Where did he go and what did he do for relief? There was nothing subtle about Michael.

"Are you asking me all this because you're all gay?" he asked Michael.

"Absolutely not. I speak only for me, not the other guys. I'm just nosy," he assured Randy.

"Well," Randy said. "I'm a very private person, and I'm straight. Maybe someday I'll tell you all about me, but for now let's drop it." Michael didn't have much choice, now did he?

CHAPTER FOURTEEN

As soon as he finished lunch, Randy took off to prepare the contracts. The crew lingered a bit longer and then drove home, three to a car. Ron and Foster said they wanted to make sure they weren't needed at the store. They told the others to meet them there at 3:45. Dan's office was close by.

They got to Dan's office a little before 4:30 and he ushered them right in to a little conference room where there would be room for all of them. Knowing that Michael was the lawyer for the group, he handed him all the documents, which Michael actually read right down to the small print.

"It looks good to me," he announced to the room in general. Then Dan had each one of them come up to him one at a time in the order that their name appeared on the contracts. He pointed out all the various places they had to sign. It took several minutes for each crew member to do their thing, and when they were through, Dan handed Michael a copy of all the documents. Then, he took all the certified checks for the balance of the down payment. The check from Jeff's bank had arrived two days earlier.

"Well," he said as he went around the table shaking hands, "the place is yours. I took the liberty of transferring all the utilities into Jeff's name at his office address. I don't want to be presumptuous, but you told me he was the official accountant for you guys. The only thing I couldn't transfer was the telephone, but I'm leaving that to you guys if you even want a land phone. I'm sure you all have cells."

Jeff got up and gave Dan a hug. "That's just fine he said. "Dan, we can't thank you enough. You've gone way above and beyond for us."

Just then there was a knock on the door, and Randy came in armed with a load of papers. He dropped the papers on the conference room table and went over to Dan and engulfed him in a bear hug. "Hi Uncle Dan," he said.

"Dan's your uncle?" Michael asked.

"Only by injection," Randy joked. "Warren's my blood uncle."

"That's why I gave you more than one contractor's name, Foster, and kept my relationship with Randy quiet. I didn't want you to accuse me of nepotism." Dan interjected. "I'll leave you guys now with your contractor. I'll be outside if you need me," he added.

As Michael reviewed the contract, Randy and Foster referred to the blueprints and when Michael and Foster approved the deal, the signing began again. Jeff prepared a check for $1,650, the 10% Randy had requested and gave it to him.

"One thing good about a small town," Randy said. "Everyone is either related or at least knows each other. On the way down here, I stopped at the County Clerk's office with the blueprints and drew down the permits. The fees were included in my price so it's all taken care of. I expect to start work on Wednesday morning."

The crew gave up one loud cheer, and Dan ran in to see what was happening. "It's cool, Unc," Randy said. "I think I have some happy clients here."

"What are you guys doing for dinner tonight?" Dan asked as Randy started to gather up his papers.

Ron answered. "Well we have sort of made Joey's our unofficial dinner place, but this week I haven't made reservations yet.

"I don't think you'll need them this time of year, but I'll call anyway. I need a head count first," Dan said. Ron called his parents, who declined this time so it would only be the six of them, Dan and Warren. Michael looked at Randy, and asked hopefully, "How about you, Randy?"

"Sorry guys, not this time. I have a date. I'll see you next weekend." He left with all his papers and Michael turned right to Dan.

"Is he or isn't he?" he wanted to know.

"Stay cool, Michael. Last I heard he was as straight as an arrow," Dan informed them.

All Michael could say was, "Shit, all the good ones are straight."

They all laughed at the twist of an old joke. They agreed to meet Dan and Warren at Joey's at 7 PM. It was already 6 PM. With all their business concluded, they went home to refresh themselves and get ready for dinner.

Joey greeted them like old friends, and this time added, "Welcome to the neighborhood." He seemed to know everything that was going on in the town. Who needs a newspaper?

"Thanks," they all said at the same time.

They all had a decadent, delicious dinner, and when it came time to pay, the check had been taken care of by Dan. The crew put up a sincere stink and wanted to pay their share, but Dan informed them that he always took out his clients after a closing. He was deaf to the argument that they were six for the earning of only one commission. There was nothing they could do but hug Dan and Warren goodnight and head for home.

During dinner, the temperature had really plummeted. They immediately turned on the space heater. The night before, the living room had gotten comfortably warm in a few minutes. Tonight, it got warmer, but was still chilly. They decided to move the coffee table and set up the sleeping bags on the living room floor, two to a bag.

When each couple was snuggled in their private cocoons, they talked for a while and agreed that until the cabin was heated, they would get up early on Sunday mornings. They would meet at Denny's for breakfast and drive up for the day to check on things. They would try to get home before 10 PM.

Ron said, "That sounds like a plan to me, but I do have a request. I'm not a religious fanatic, but I would like to get here by 10 AM so I can make church. It's very important to my folks."

"Not a problem," Michael murmured. That was an important statement coming from Michael. He was totally agnostic.

The next morning they could not ignore the fact that they had to shower and shave as well as perform other morning duties. Jeff and Jim had kitchen duty so the others moved the space heater as close to the bathroom as they could to get the room as warm as possible. They used the shower two at a time, but could only shave one at a time. Eventually everyone was ready and dressed for church. They sat at the kitchen table and Jeff served eggs, toast and coffee. They all helped to clean up, and off they went to the Fishers.

Josie Fisher greeted them all with a kiss on the cheek and told them how handsome they all looked. That was no lie. The Fishers got in Ron's car with Ron and Foster. Jeff and Jim got into Michael's car with Michael and Jerry, and followed Ron to the church. The sun had warmed the air a lot and many congregants were standing in front of the church socializing before the service. The crew was happy to see Joey, Rosie, Dan and Warren, Joe Torrance, and Randy. Randy was holding on to the cutest little girl of about five years.

Joe Torrance came over first and grabbed Foster's hand and welcomed him to 'his' church. It was his way of saying that there were no hard feelings, and to welcome the crew as neighbors. Foster was surprised and exceptionally pleased.

Michael made his way over to Randy. "I know you are a very private person, but you've got to tell me who this lovely lady is on your arm. Was she your date last night?"

Randy nodded yes. "Liz," he said, "this here's Michael Costello. He's got his eye on you, but don't even think of getting married for another fifteen years. You better listen to your father."

"So this is your little girl. She must take after her mother who I don't see anywhere," Michael looked around. Randy's face darkened. He picked up his daughter and said, "Come darling, let's go inside."

Michael's big mouth often got him in trouble. His mother referred to it as 'his big fat lawyer's mouth.' But for the life of him, he couldn't figure out what he had done this time. Warren was talking to Jeff so he ran over and interrupted them. He told Warren what had happened and wanted to know if he had done something wrong so he could apologize.

"Shit," Warren said. "Nobody ever talks about his wife. She married Randy on the rebound after her lover was sentenced to life in prison for murder. He was a no good son of a bitch, but Elizabeth loved him. Well, one day there's a knock on Elizabeth's back door, and when she opens the door, there stands Lou the low life. He had escaped from prison and wanted her to go with him to Los Angeles, where they could get lost in the crowds. He had stolen a car and he gave her about two minutes to decide. She threw some clothes in a bag and went with him, leaving little Liz, who was about six months old, alone in the house.

"A little way out of town, a state trooper picked up on the stolen car and started after them. Lou tried to out run him and ended up piling into a very old, very sturdy tree. He was killed outright. Elizabeth lived for a few hours, just long enough to let us know what happened."

"My God," Michael was truly sorry for his big mouth right now. He ran into the church. Most of the crowd was still outside so he spotted Randy easily. He slid into the seat next to him, and mumbled, "I am truly sorry, man. I didn't know."

"It's OK," Randy said. "You couldn't have known." Then he did something really surprising. He took Michael's hand and squeezed it. When he released Michael's hand, Michael patted Randy on his shoulder and left to join his friends.

As he walked to the rear of the church, he saw his friends coming in. They took almost the entire rear row. He joined them, and found himself with Jerry on one side of him and Ron on the other. He leaned over to Ron and asked, "What denomination is this church? Jeff, Jim and I were born Catholics and Jerry is Jewish. Will it be all right?"

"Don't worry, man," Ron answered. "The church is non-denominational. Did you notice that it's simply called, 'The Summer Street Church of God?' I think you'll all be comfortable here.

A few minutes later, a comely woman started to play the organ and a six member choir climbed the stairs and stood behind the speaker's lectern. Then the pastor came to the lectern. "Good morning everyone," he said. He looked around, and smiling at all the new people, he said, "I see lots of fresh faces here this morning. Welcome to you all. I'm Pastor Patterson, and I hope to say hello to all of you after the service. There will be refreshments in the social hall as usual. Now please turn to page 38 in your hymnal."

The organ began to play and the congregation began to sing. The newbies examined the pastor. He was in his early forties. He stood about five feet, ten inches tall, and weighed no more than 150 pounds. He wore no vestments at all, but was dressed in an ill fitting business suit. In spite of the ill fit, Pastor Patterson was a very good looking man. They all looked into his eyes. They were a soft hazel color and they were looking over his flock with such love that anyone coming into the sanctuary would be struck by the vibes of affection that permeated the church. Never had Michael, for one, ever been in the presence of a man like this. Michael wanted to hug him and beg for his love and for his compassion. He could not explain his feeling.

When the sermon began they were all blown away. The pastor spoke of man's need to love one another, not just family and friends, but neighbors, elected officials, people who are different than you are, and most important, your enemies. "When you can love your enemies," he challenged his flock. "they will no longer be enemies. Hatred and wars will disappear from the planet." He continued, "Love is the most potent force in God's universe. Never forget that." There was not one word uttered about sin and sinners and going to hell or homosexuals being damned. Love, only love.

Michael and Jerry were of different faiths. They had discussed their religious differences and realized they had none. Both had believed that their religions offered nothing but hypocrisy and had long wandered from them. They looked at each other now and they were both crying.

The service ended and Pastor Patterson invited everyone to the social hall. The newbies were anxious to meet him and tell him how inspiring his service was.

Out of some primal need, Michael and Jerry reached him first. They enveloped him in a bear hug and thanked him profusely for his inspiration and for his love. The rest of the crew observed this display of affection in utter awe. The pastor returned their hugs, and asked that they call him, Paul. He chatted with them for a few minutes and they promised him that he would see them again. Then he excused himself to greet the rest of his flock.

Michael could not move. He just stood there trying to suppress his racking sobs. Suddenly he felt something tugging at his pant leg. He looked down to see little Liz. She looked up at him with big blue eyes and said, "I like you Mr. Costello. You're a nice man."

During the social hour, Paul managed to spend a few minutes with everyone there. Jeff told him that they would be there every Sunday until their addition was finished. After that, the cabin would be heated and they would come for full weekends and vacations, whenever possible. Chances were that even if all of them couldn't come at the same time, two of them would be there. Sometimes, his dad and his godfather might come for fishing and he would be sure to tell them to come meet Pastor Paul, even though they were Catholics. As they said goodbye to Paul, each crew member shook his hand. Later they compared notes and they all had the same reaction. As he took their hands, they each felt a powerful surge of energy permeate their bodies. Jerry described it as a powerful laser light of healing. No wonder Ron and Foster had requested that they all get there in time for church.

Jeff was determined that there would be no obstacles to their weekly trips to 'their little piece of heaven.' The first thing Monday morning, he went out and traded his Saturn Ion on a Plymouth Grand Voyager which comfortably seated seven people. Then he went to the bank with Michael and they opened the 'cabin joint account' with the remaining mortgage money. Both he and Michael could sign checks. The first check they wrote was to reimburse Jeff for everything he had laid out on behalf of the crew. They were now all on an even keel.

CHAPTER FIFTEEN

The following Sunday morning at 7 AM, Michael and Jerry parked their car in a guest space at Jeff's and Jim's condo. This was the last weekend that Ron and Foster would be going up early to help in his parents' store until next April. The following Sunday they would all travel there together. They had begun to refer to the cabin as their 'little piece of heaven.'

There was no luggage to place in the car as they expected to be home the same night. They drove to their favorite Denny's for breakfast and then headed upstate. Their first stop was the Fisher's home. When they arrived, they all hugged and kissed, and Jeff asked if they had been to the cabin.

"Not yet," Ron said, "We were waiting for you guys to arrive."

"We were waiting for you also," Jason said. "We can all go check it out right after church services." He looked at his watch and said, "We ought to get going." When they got outside and saw Jeff's new van, they made quite a fuss over it. Jeff showed them all the bells and whistles of the fully loaded vehicle. Ron and Foster went with his parents and the other four went in Jeff's new van.

When they arrived at the church, they saw that the crowd was considerably lighter than last week, and they figured that many summer residents had closed down their cabins for the season. Michael and Jerry spotted Randy and Liz and ran over. This time they all hugged each other warmly. Michael picked up Liz and gave her a big smack of a kiss on her cheek. She started to giggle. "You tickled me," she said. Michael made a mental note to shave every Sunday morning. He was not in the habit of shaving during the weekend at all.

Randy wanted to know if they had been out to the cabin. Michael said they would go after church, and Randy said that he would meet them there. In the mean time the others were milling through the crowd greeting everyone they knew. Finally they all went into the sanctuary and found seats. The organist and the choir found their places and Pastor Paul came out and stood at the lectern. Michael was pleased to see that the suit he was wearing fit him much better this Sunday, and he appeared even more handsome.

When the congregation began to sing the first hymn, the crew sang joyfully and loudly. They felt more at home this week and joined in whole heartedly with all the others. They had each made a subconscious decision that this was going to be their church from now on.

This week's sermon concerned nit picking the bible to find little snippets of verse to use for bigotry. "God is all about love," Paul told his flock, "and to use his name to support bigotry and hate was to deny his love for us all." The homosexuals listening to him knew exactly what he meant. Michael knew in his heart that this sermon was for the benefit of Paul's new church members.

During the social hour, Jerry managed to get Paul aside. "Can I talk to you for a minute?" he asked.

"Sure, son. What's up?"

Jerry cleared his throat. It was evident it was going to be hard for him to say what he wanted to. "Speak up, Jerry. I don't bite and I certainly don't judge."

Jerry got his courage up. He cleared his throat again and began speaking. "You must realize that Michael and I are life partners. Even though he refers to himself as a terminal catholic, he is still pretty much rooted in catholic dogma. He loves me but fears for my soul, not because we are gay, but because I am not baptized. I thought maybe, since we plan on being members of your church, you would instruct me in your religion, and baptize me."

Paul put his arm around Jerry's shoulder and laughed. "Jerry, he said, "There is no dogma in my church. All you need do is accept that God exists and that he loves you as he does all his children. I'd be honored to baptize you. How about we surprise everyone next Sunday?"

"That would be great," Jerry answered. "Let's keep it our little secret."

"Who would you like to be your godparents?" Paul asked.

Jerry thought for a minute and said, "I guess the Fishers."

"Wonderful," Paul said. "We can even surprise them. At the proper time, I'll call on them to come to the baptismal font and be your godparents. I don't think there will be a problem. In fact I can guarantee they'll be thrilled. Now we had better join the others."

The crew thought that they, the Fishers, Randy and Liz would be the only ones caravanning to the cabin, but they soon realized that half the church congregation followed them. There was Rosie, Joey, Dan and Warren, Pastor Paul, several friends of the Fishers, and a few others that only Ron knew.

They were shocked when they got there. Randy's construction crew had only worked on the place for four days. The guys were unprepared for so much progress. The back porch and the dining room wall were gone. The new wall, however, was framed out. The studs were in place as was a clearly visible space for the door which would lead to the new wing. The concrete slab had been poured, and about half the new structure had been framed out. You could actually get a feel for what the place would look like. Randy assured them that by next Sunday, the wing would be all closed in, the roof would be on and the siding would be in place. Then weather would not be a factor because all the remaining work would be indoors. Foster looked at the work from a more professional viewpoint and he was pleased that he had chosen Randy. Every part of the construction was first rate work. Everything was done far beyond code requirements.

The rest of the folks oohed and aahed, and then most of them left to go home. The crew, the Fishers, Dan, Warren, Randy, Liz, and last but not least, Paul, drove to Rosie's for lunch. Michael wanted to ask Paul some personal questions, but he decided to hold his tongue, just as he had with Jeff in regard to his fathers. If Paul had something to tell them, and if he ever wanted to, Michael was certain that he would.

During the lunch, Michael found himself sitting next to Dan so he took the opportunity to ask him about Paul. Dan told him that Paul had a ministry, coincidentally, in St. Paul, Minn. About three years ago, his wife passed away. They never had children and Paul wanted to live in a new place without a lot of sad memories, so he answered their ad for a new minister, and here he is. Dan added, "He sure has made a big change in our church service, all to the better. The folks all love him and approve of his philosophy about life. I think that's why our town is so liberal and so accepting of diversity. Thank God and thank Pastor Paul."

After lunch the crew all headed back to the Fishers to hang out and everyone else went home. Josie informed them that she had made dinner for all which she would serve early about 5:30. They could all be started for home before 7 and would certainly get home by 9. The men started to object, but she would hear none of it.

They started for home in very high spirits. The cabin addition was proceeding nicely, and they felt really confident that it was all in Randy's very capable hands. They also noted that next weekend they would all be sharing a ride and that made them feel good too. They hated being separated. They treasured every moment they shared as a family.

Jeff dropped Michael and Jerry off at their car in the parking lot and they all kissed good night. Jeff could not help but notice that Jerry had a silly grin on his face, but dismissed it as a case of fatigue.

When they got upstairs and locked the door. Jeff and Jim embraced warmly. "I've missed your kisses," Jim said. "Me too," Jeff echoed. In minutes they were in the shower together. They took joy in washing each other's bodies. Each one knew exactly where his partner's erogenous zones were and concentrated on getting those areas meticulously clean in anticipation of what was to come.

When they were in bed together, Jeff climbed on top of Jim in a sixty nine position. They found each other's cocks and begin tickling their shafts with their tongues. Jeff moved slightly forward so he could kiss Jim's balls and Jim's 'hot spot' between his balls and the crack of his ass. He couldn't quite reach Jim's love hole in this position, but he was doing enough to drive Jim wild, and Jim was doing all he could to reciprocate. Usually when they felt their climaxes approaching they would stop their partner and hold back the orgasm. Tonight, they were so lost in ecstasy that both just let it happen. Jim came first and Jeff got so busy trying to drink down all his spunk, he temporarily lost his own feeling of relief, but just for a few seconds, and then he came in great gushes, and Jim gobbled him all up. They lay still for a while and then Jeff turned around to face Jim. Their lips and cocks met, and before they knew it, they were fast asleep.

Early on Friday morning, when he was alone in his office, Jerry called Paul to discuss the baptism and to tell him that he wanted to pay for the food in the social hall after the service. Paul didn't argue that offer at all.

Paul said that he had not put a notice in the church bulletin that there was going to be a baptism that Sunday. He was just going to make the announcement at the proper time, and then call him and the Fishers up to the pulpit. He'd give everyone a moment to get over the shock and then he would perform the simple rite. When he invited everyone to the social hall after the service, as he always did, he would ask them to attend as guests of Jerry Rubin.

They chatted for a few minutes like old friends, and suddenly Jerry felt comfortable enough to say something to Paul. "Dan told me about your wife's passing back in St. Paul," he said, "and I wanted to tell you how sorry I am." There was a long silence and Jerry regretted opening his big, fat mouth. "I'm sorry for getting so personal," he said. "Please forgive me."

"There's nothing to forgive," Paul said. "I was just sitting here trying to make a decision and I've made it. I want to tell you something. And I want you to know that it isn't a secret, if you want to tell your friends. When I applied for the position of pastor of this wonderful church, my résumé said that I was a recent widower. That was true, but the church board assumed that my wife had passed, when in fact it was my partner of nearly twenty years. He was my whole life, Jerry. He died of a brain tumor. Not a day goes by that I don't miss him and mourn for him. I didn't exactly lie, and when everyone thought I had lost my wife, I just didn't correct the misconception. I knew that everyone accepted Dan and Warren and Ron and Foster, but they were all life time residents and I was a stranger and a minister, so I said nothing, and nobody ever discussed 'her.' Then when I met you fellows, and I saw how loving and accepting everyone was, and how honest you all were with the residents here, I've now decided to come out."

Jerry was stunned, but Michael had hinted to him that his gaydar was suspicious, and Jerry knew that Michael would be pleased. Of course, he couldn't tell Michael anything until after the baptism. Michael's legal eagle mind would want to know why Jerry had had a conversation with Paul.

"Thank you for sharing that with me, but if you don't mind Paul, I'll keep it our secret until after the baptism. Also, I don't think I should out you. You'll have to do it yourself. And for what it's worth, I don't think it will make a damn bit of difference to your congregation."

CHAPTER SIXTEEN

Early Sunday morning, the plan was to pick up Ron and Foster first and then Michael and Jerry. Michael, and Jerry crept into the third set of seats in the rear of the van. Ron and Foster were seated in the middle bucket seats. Jeff drove and Jim rode shot gun. Their regular Denny's was out of the way, but they stopped at a coffee shop located just before the main highway. They were too excited to eat so they ordered coffee and some Danish pastry and got going as soon as possible. At 7:45 AM they entered the highway. Within five minutes everyone fell asleep except the driver. Jeff put the radio on to keep him company and still nobody woke up.

At 9:35, Jeff pulled onto the Fisher's long driveway which ran to the right of the general store and continued to their house behind the store. He stopped the car, and still everyone slept, so he got out quietly and knocked on the Fishers door. Jason opened immediately, but his face went pale when he saw that Jeff was alone.

"What's wrong?" he asked afraid of the answer.

"Nothing's wrong." Jeff smiled his infectious smile. "They're all asleep. Tell you what, I'll drive right on to the church and you can follow."

"Boy, will they be surprised," Jason smiled.

The driveway curved in front of the house so that any car could pull out facing the road. Jeff was able to get back on the road quickly and was at the church in a few minutes. The usual regulars were milling about and Jeff went to hug and greet them all. He recruited all his friends, including the pastor, to surround the car and yell as loudly as possible, "Good morning America."

Little Liz Jones was laughing hysterically. That did it. Everyone woke up. It took a moment to realize that they had arrived, and little by little they exited the car. Liz took Michael's hand and said, 'I think they're sick Mr. Costello. Should we call 911?"

Pastor Paul was chatting with Jerry when he broke away and entered the church. This seemed to be a signal for those not already inside to come in for the service.

Soon the organ began to play and the choir took their positions. Paul came out wearing a brand new suit. His hair was newly cut, and to tell the truth, he looked quite dapper and very handsome. The whole congregation could not help but smile and some of them wondered if he had something special in mind today. He asked his flock to turn to a hymn on page 372 of their hymnals. It was written by an unknown composer just a few years ago and nobody had heard it nor were they familiar with it. It would be up to the choir to get them into the melody. It was called 'Beginnings.'

The choir had never sounded better. They began to sing softly about the birth of love for God and for one another. The melody was ethereal, hauntingly beautiful. "As love grows so does the spirit, and brings us closer to God," they sang as their voices rose into a crescendo. A few tissues came out to wipe away the tears. Jerry was sobbing like a baby, and Michael could only wonder what was up with him.

Paul rose to speak and the flock expected to hear his usual thoughts on the power of love. Instead he began to explain the importance of baptism. "It was intended to wipe away the original sin of conception," he opined. "But I don't believe that an act as beautiful as conception could be sin. When God creates a new life, that is glory of the highest order, never sin. No, I believe that baptism symbolically washes clean our old lives, and brings us into a bright new life in which God is our constant shepherd."

Jerry's body was now racked with sobbing and Michael could only put his arm around him in what seemed to be a useless effort to comfort him.

Paul spoke a bit more on the cleansing and healing effects of baptism. Then he paused and smiled at the congregation. "I have a surprise for you this beautiful morning. We have a baptism to perform today." He raised his voice when he made this announcement and smiled broadly at the congregants. They all looked around expecting to see a new born baby somewhere in the church, but none was present.

"Will Jerry Rubin please come forward," he called out to Jerry. Jerry stood up with wobbly legs, and virtually ran to the pulpit. He thought that if he walked slower, his legs would buckle out from under him. Michael's jaw just dropped. For once, he was totally speechless. It was a good thing this was a church and not a court room.

Jerry stood beside Paul who put his arm around him and smiled. Then he looked at the congregation again, spotted the Fishers and said, "Jason and Josie Fisher, Jerry would consider it a great honor if you would stand as his godparents at the portal of his new and wonderful life." The Fishers were stunned, but managed to find their way to the pulpit. When they got there they embraced Jerry, literally taking his breath away.

The pastor then performed a very non traditional, merely symbolic baptism. When he was through, he too embraced Jerry, and whispered to everyone to stay where they were. He motioned to the organist and she began to play 'Climb Every Mountain' from Carousel. The choir began to sing and the congregation joined in. Somewhere half way through the song, Michael could constrain himself no longer. He ran to the altar and enveloped Jerry in a very chaste and manly bear hug. Then all the members of the crew ran up and embraced Jerry in turn.

While hugging Jerry, Ron whispered in his ear, "We're brothers now. We'll have to cut out the incest." Jerry whispered back, "Not on your life. We know certain people who haven't been stopped by incest." They broke away from each other smiling.

When the song ended, Paul had to shoo everyone back to their seats. When order was restored, he continued. "As usual we will have refreshments in the social hall after the service. Today, the food has been catered by our own Rosie Kelly and is a gift from our beloved baptismal boy, Jerry Rubin." The congregation applauded. The choir led them in a final joyous hymn, and Paul bade them all to go in peace and with love in their hearts. He walked to the entrance of the church and greeted everyone as they proceeded to the social hall.

The crew usually went to Rosie's for lunch after church, but today Rosie brought the lunch to them. There were bowls of mixed salad greens, shrimp salad, tuna salad and chicken salad, an assortment of breads, rolls, and bagels, and fruit salad for dessert. The buffet table was well equipped with plastic plates, bowls and flatware. On a table against the wall there was a cooler full of soft drinks, and two large urns with regular and decaf coffee.

Sugar, sweeteners, and cream were also in plentiful supply. Jeff and Jim were busy crunching numbers and concluded that this was going to cost Jerry a pretty penny.

That gave Jeff an idea. He went around the room, speaking to all the new friends and buddies he had met here. He was taking a head count of who wanted to go to Joey's Place for dinner. He made sure that the Fishers had not planned on feeding everyone. Of course, the crew was definitely going. Jeff didn't give the Fishers an opportunity to say no to celebrate their godson's baptism. Randy couldn't accept quickly enough for him and Liz (unless he could get a sitter on short notice.) Paul, Dan and Warren also accepted. Jeff called Joey's place and made a 5:30 reservation for thirteen people. Then he went over to where Joey and Rosie were huddled in conversation. He gave Joey a heads up about the large reservation.

Little by little the congregants left the social hall. Rosie's cleanup crew arrived and Foster told Randy they were ready to go to the construction site. Randy remembered he had a daughter. He picked her up and he and Liz headed for Randy's pickup truck. Ron and Foster went with Ron's parents, and Paul went with Jeff, Jim, Michael and Jerry. Dan and Warren went in their car.

When they arrived at the cabin, the crew all uttered together, "OMG!" Just as Randy had promised the entire house was closed in. The roof and siding were completed, and from the outside, at least, the cabin not only looked huge, but it looked finished. The crew would have to stop referring to it as a cabin, and refer to it as their country home.

Everyone went inside. The old section had the new heating ducts running along the ceilings. The vents were clearly visible. It was otherwise relatively untouched.

"The ducts will be covered with drywall, and form soffits. We'll be able to cover them with bric a brac," Foster explained. They walked into the new wing through the doorless frame. All the studs were in place and the electrical wiring was already installed. The outlets were affixed to the studs.

The new furnace was installed and there was a new circuit breaker in the furnace room.

"The old breaker won't be needed in the kitchen anymore so we'll close it up and have more wall space," Foster explained. He was treating this small addition as one of his major architectural projects. He was so proud and happy at the way it was developing.

Randy added, "After next weekend, you can start picking paint colors and you can start buying new furniture and carpeting." This prompted the crew, the Fishers and Paul to begin a discussion on decorating and furnishing. Josie let the newbies know that there was a Sears and a Walmart about three miles further up the road past Rosie's. She suggested that they might want to visit the stores next weekend.

The crew hung out at the Fishers all afternoon, and Paul remained with them. Actually he led a lonely life and these people were becoming like a family to him. In the future he would always be welcome to join them in family affairs. Josie kept the coffee pot going, and Rosie had urged everyone to take home some leftovers, so Josie put out some pastries also. The coffee got consumed but nobody ate the pastries. They were saving their appetites for Joey's.

During the afternoon both Jason and Josie kept coming over to Jerry and hugging him. They had never been godparents before and it was like they wanted to make up for the twenty four years they had missed. As for Paul, this was the first baptism he had performed since he came to the community. He was pretty excited himself. He too kept hugging Jerry, and Michael's gaydar was going bing, bing, bing. As for Michael, all he could think of was what baptismal gifts he could give the love of his life when they got home tonight. His imagination began to work overtime, and he knew it would be a while before he could stand up without embarrassing himself.

The afternoon passed all too soon. The love and warmth that filled this house made it difficult for everyone to want to leave. Finally Josie announced that it was time to go to Joey's. The mid autumn sun was setting earlier every day, and it was nearly dark when they got into the cars. Again Ron and Foster went with the Fishers, and Paul went with the rest of the crew,

Joey greeted them with warm handshakes, but he gave Jerry a big hug and a broad smile. Randy was there already, but no Liz. Obviously Randy had gotten a sitter. Michael was disappointed. There was a special bond growing between him and Liz, but of course he wasn't aware of it yet. They were barely seated at the extra long table Joey had provided, when Dan and Warren came in also. Joey assigned two waiters and two bus boys to serve them. The waiters brought over two pitchers of beer, and informed them that the beer was on the house and refills were also part of the gift to Jerry. Joey wanted to give them wine, but he knew the crew well enough by now to know that everybody preferred beer with a barbequed meal. They all thanked Joey profusely as the waiters handed out menus. After the orders were taken, Michael stood up and asked everyone to fill their glasses.

"I want to make a toast," he said. "Here's to the handsomest, most wonderful guy in the world. He makes my life a total joy. He's the reason I get up in the morning and the reason I can rest my head at night. Today he made me the happiest guy in the world, because now I know that we will not only spend this lifetime together, but we'll be together for all eternity."

"Here, here!" everyone said as they raised their glasses and sipped the beer. Paul was crying like a baby. He was sitting next to Josie who put her arm around his shoulder and pulled him toward her. Jerry knew that he was mourning for his deceased lover. The hopeless romantic that dwelled within him tried to think of someone appropriate to introduce to Paul. Nobody came to mind immediately.

Ron saw that it was getting late. He wanted to get on the road soon. After all tomorrow was a work day. He asked one of the waiters for the check and was informed that Mr. Simmons had taken care of it. Ron started to object, but Jeff stopped him. "This is our gift to Jerry," he said. This has been an unbelievable day and Jim and I want to celebrate it with Jerry and Michael. Don't forget we have known them longer than any of you, and it is truly our pleasure."

They all drove to the Fishers. Randy was going to drop Paul off on his way home, and Ron and Foster were getting back in the van. It took at least fifteen minutes for all the goodbye hugs and kisses, and Michael saw Paul kiss Jerry on the lips. He vowed to have a talk with Jerry on the matter.

Traffic was light and they made excellent time back to Phoenix. Jeff dropped Ron and Foster off first, and when they said goodnight, Ron couldn't help but say to Jerry, "I'll see you at lunch tomorrow, BRO!" But he got so emotional, his voice cracked when he said it.

Michael and Jerry were next to be dropped off, and Jeff and Jim couldn't wait to get home, shower and go to sleep. Go to sleep they did. They were too tired for anything else.

At the Costello/Rubin household things were different. He and Jerry went into their bedroom and in minutes they were naked in bed. They didn't give a damn that they hadn't showered since that morning. Their lips and tongues locked in battle. Their hard as rock erections ground against each other.

"Fuck me, Michael. Fuck me hard. If I don't feel you inside of me soon, I'll die and I'll go to heaven." Jim added the last phrase in jest, and got Michael giggling. Nevertheless, Michael took the lube off his night table as Jerry got into position. He generously lubed Jerry's ass and his own cock, and guided himself into Jerry's waiting well. When Michael was all the way in and Jerry was filled to his satisfaction, Michael leaned forward. His abdomen dry humped Jerry's eager prick and their lips were locked together in long and tender passionate kisses. They lay that way for a longtime, neither wishing to move and spoil the moment. But after a while nature got the best of them. Michael began to stroke in and out, in and out. While he did that, his fingers found Jerry's nipples and he began to gently pinch them. Michael's abdomen rubbing Jerry's cock, and now the tweaking nipples were too much for Jerry. Michael could sense that Jerry was close. He shifted position slightly, knowing that his cock would now graze against Jerry's prostate. That did it. With a shout that the neighbors had to hear, Jerry let loose his cum. It smeared between them so that they were nearly stuck together. When Jerry came he involuntarily constricted his ass and that put Michael over the top. He came screaming even louder than Jerry. He had never before experienced such an intense orgasm. He counted at least eight spasms of ejecting semen, before he collapsed on top of Jerry. They lay that way for a long time. Jerry's hands kept running up and down Michael's back and cupping and caressing Michael's bubble butt. Finally, Michael rolled off Jerry, and they fell asleep.

When they got up the next morning, it was later than usual. They showered, shaved, and you know what, as quickly as possible. Once dressed, they went into the kitchen. They had no time for breakfast, but they each had a glass of orange juice, and went off to work.

The crew arrived at the Fisher's home on Sunday as usual, with about fifteen minutes to spare before church. Hugs and welcome kisses abounded before they headed out for the church. They must have been a little later than usual because everybody was already inside.

Michael looked around as the crew and the Fishers entered the church. They didn't get a chance to say hello to anyone until the social hour. As usual, Paul greeted each of his flock as they left the sanctuary to go to the social hall. He shook most hands, but each crew member got a really strong bear hug from him. Liz spotted Michael as he entered the social hall. She jumped up into his arms and kissed him on the cheek.

After some coffee and Danish they all headed to the cabin. This time it was just the crew, Randy and Liz. The others said they had checked on progress during the week and would pass today.

The crew whistled when they got there. It's easier at this point to say what wasn't finished. The new bathroom needed to be tiled. That included the walls and the floors. The bedrooms were complete except for the wood trim work and the painting. Randy said that Josie had chosen the colors and the tiles during the week so if they didn't like it, it was her fault. He said that samples were on the kitchen table for them to approve. The new outside deck also needed to be constructed. The furniture and new springs and mattresses were coming right after the painting was completed and the carpeting was installed. Randy estimated that the cabin would be completed and he would have a CO in three weeks, just in time for Thanksgiving. This pleased everyone and they gave out a loud whoopee.

"Now let's go to Rosie's before I faint," Foster said. He hadn't eaten anything at the social hour, saving his appetite for lunch.

"Yay," Liz said, giggling.

After lunch, Randy invited the crew to hang out at his place. Ron called his folks to tell them that they were all hanging out at Randy's place, and they were invited to join them. Josie declined and told them that she was making dinner for the crew and the Joneses. She would not take no for an answer this time. They had given Joey enough of their business and would no doubt give him much more. She told them all to be there at 5PM so they could get going for home at a decent hour.

The days flew by too quickly. The cabin was indeed ready the weekend before Thanksgiving and the crew drove up to Lake Henry on the Sunday before Thanksgiving to see it. As they had agreed a while ago, they would stop referring to it as a cabin and would begin to call it their country home. It was beautiful, and Jeff announced that there was a good sum of money remaining in the joint account. It would be a while before the crew would need to contribute additional funds for mortgage payments, provisions and so on.

Much to their chagrin, the crew could not use the country home over the Thanksgiving holiday, for a variety of reasons, mostly family commitments. Their first weekend would have to be the one following Thanksgiving.

The Friday after Thanksgiving Weekend, the crew all left work a little earlier than usual. Michael, Jerry, Jim and Jeff not only packed for the weekend but also packed stuff they wanted to leave in their country home as Ron and Foster had already done. When they arrived in Lake Henry they made a quick stop to say hello to the Fishers and an even quicker stop to say hello to Randy. Liz didn't want them to go, but they all assured her that they would see plenty of each other over the weekend.

They arrived at their home and unpacked. Michael and Jerry took the bedroom they had used in the past and Jeff and Jim did the same. Ron and Foster had already taken the far bedroom of the new wing which had a window view of the lake.

Because they were tired from the trip and it was growing late, they decided to go to Joey's for dinner even though the house was well supplied. Joey greeted them warmly, and provided the usual wonderful barbequed meal. They ate and ran. Each was anxious to "break in" the new house.

When they had arrived the afternoon sun had warmed the house, but now it was quite chilly. Ron turned up the thermostat, and delicious warm air started to blow through the virgin vents. In no time the place was toasty and the crew decided to strip. Once settled in the living room, Michael popped a porno tape into the new VCR and TV set. After a few minutes of viewing hot male sex, the boys were all sporting boners. Hands started to grope, mouths started to suck, assholes began to receive fingers and then cocks. Everyone was moaning and groaning in delightful pleasure. When everybody began to cum, Ron found himself with Jim. Jeff found himself with Michael and Jerry and Foster came in each other's mouths. The mixed couples lay in each others arms, hands on cocks for a long while. Finally Jerry said, "Hey guys, I'm falling asleep. I'm going to bed."

Everyone agreed that the house had been properly 'broken in,' and headed for their bedrooms. Ron took it on himself to turn the thermostat down a couple of degrees for the night and lock up the house.

Jeff was in bed when Jim joined him. "This mattress Josie picked out is so firm and comfortable and it doesn't creak," he told Jim. Jim literally jumped into bed and the mattress made not a sound. They immediately coupled and started to make out. Jeff's cock was deeply imbedded in Jim's mouth when he realized that they were undisturbed by noises from the next room. Only when either Jerry or Michael came did they hear a slight scream. If they weren't listening for it, they might have missed it.

The night ended with each couple making love to his own partner and falling into a deep and peaceful sleep. If it is true that home is where the heart is, they were indeed at home.

CHAPTER SEVENTEEN

Michael has a younger sister, who married a dead beat. They had been married for less than a year when Michelle asked her brother to handle her divorce. As a result she was in his office often during the renovation of the country home. Michael, of course, described the serenity and beauty of the place to her. On the day her divorce became final she told Michael, that she was taking a week off from her nursing job at the Mayo Clinic in Scottsdale, and asked if she could use the country place during the week. She just needed to be alone for a few days and come down from her high level of stress.

Michael checked with the crew and they were all in favor of her using the house, and the guest room in the new wing. Her intention was to go up on Tuesday morning and return Friday afternoon so as not to disturb the weekly routine of her brother and his friends. Michael gave her directions to the Fishers and told her to pick up the key there, and they would give her driving directions to the house. He also called the Fishers and told them to expect her.

Michelle arrived about 10 AM and had no trouble finding the Fishers. They welcomed her warmly, and insisted she stay for lunch, and then she could follow them to the house. They told her that they looked in on it during the week to make sure everything was all right. The Fishers were so sweet and so insistent that Michelle had to say yes. Josie dragged out some picture albums and proceeded to show her old photographs of Ron when he was a little boy. Michelle had met Ron on several occasions, and had lamented many times that he was gay.

While she was enjoying the pictures, Jason went into the other room and made a call. He just had a hunch. Michelle was as beautiful as Michael was handsome, and he was not above a little match making. Just as they were sitting down to lunch, Randy Jones just happened to drop by to say hello.

The very size of Randy knocked Michelle for a loop. It took awhile for her to realize how handsome he was as well. Jason was so right. Michelle and Randy could not take their eyes off each other. They began to chat and it was like the Fishers were not even in the room.

After lunch, it was Randy and not the Fishers, who Michelle followed to the house. He helped her bring her bags into the house and showed her to the guest room. Then he turned on the breakers that the boys shut when the house was closed up. It was chilly in the house and he turned up the thermostat for her. She thanked him profusely, and even though she had come here to be alone, she hated to see him leave.

Randy was generally very shy, but he determined not to be shy this time. He wanted this woman badly so he screwed up his courage and asked her if she would please have dinner with him this evening. This was no time for Michelle to be coy either, and she accepted immediately. At lunch she had learned about Liz so she asked if Liz could join them since she was anxious to meet her. That request sealed it for Randy. He was going to make this woman his wife and that was all there was to it. No arguments, please.

He never left the house that day. The two sat and held hands and talked until Randy said, "Let's go pick up Liz at school. She's in kindergarten." They drove up to the school and when the school bell rang, Liz was one of the first out. She spotted her dad's pick up truck and ran toward it, but she slowed when she realized there was a beautiful woman sitting next to her daddy. Randy got out of the truck to greet her.

"How would you like to meet Uncle Michael's sister?" he asked. Lizzie's face brightened immediately.

"Are you going to marry her daddy so Michael will be my real uncle?" He and Michelle laughed heartily. They both already knew that marriage was a distinct possibility.

They had dinner at Randy's that evening. After dinner, Liz and Michelle had a big conference about Lizzie's bedroom. Michelle described to her just how she would like to redecorate her room, since her daddy had no flair for fashion. Liz kept hugging her and telling her how much she loved her.

After Liz went to sleep, no words were spoken between Michelle and Randy. They fell into each other's arms, and made love in Randy's bed. In the morning, after they took Liz to school, they brought Michelle's stuff back to Randy's, and closed up the house again. She never did use her brother's country house.

During the divorce, she had moved back with her folks. The first call she made was to them. She asked them to please pack up her clothes, especially her nurses uniforms, and mail them to her in care of Randolph Jones and she gave them his address. They were worried that she might be making another mistake, and they told her to go slow. She told them that she loved Randy as much as Michael loved Jerry, and she reminded them that Michael too had fallen in love at first sight.

Her next call was to the Mayo Clinic tendering her resignation. Then she called the nearest regional hospital and set up an interview for Thursday morning. They were desperate for registered nurses. Her final call was to Michael. She told him that she had not used the country house after all, and that when he arrived Friday night, she would be here with a big surprise for him. She would not tell him where she was staying.

When all the calls were made, Randy drove them to the County Hall where they applied for a marriage license. The license would be valid by Friday afternoon. At first Randy wanted to call Paul, but he decided to visit him and introduce him to Michelle. Fortunately, the pastor was at the church. When he heard that Michelle was Michael's sister, he nearly crushed her with his strong hugs. After Randy explained the reason for their visit, Paul looked at Randy and said, "You see, there was a reason that Liz took so quickly and so strongly to Michael, and started to call him Uncle right away. Your marriage was made in heaven." The happy couple beamed.

They arranged to be married Saturday morning. All the crew would be there, the Fishers, Dan and Warren. Michelle called Jeff and told him what was going on. She begged him not to tell Michael and Jerry, but to please call her folks, give them directions and make sure they got here by Friday afternoon. All of this was accomplished by 11 AM. Talk about whirlwind romances.

Randy called Rosie, gave her an approximate head count and asked her to arrange a little reception in the church social hall Saturday after the wedding. He left it entirely in her hands. "What else?" Randy asked Michelle. "Did we think of everything?"

"You go to work and make us lots of money, big guy," Michelle said. "Tell me where to go for shopping. I want to surprise Lizzie with new curtains and a comforter when she comes home today. Her bedroom should look like a little girl's room, not an institution. I'll work on our room after the wedding, when I will be able to breathe again."

Michelle insisted on picking up Lizzie after school, so Randy didn't have to interrupt his work. When she got home, her new curtains were hanging, the comforter was on her bed and 'Winnie the Pooh' pictures adorned her walls. She screeched with delight and kissed Michelle over and over again.

The crew always drove to the Fishers first when they arrived on Friday evening. They came to pick up the key to their house, but no matter how much they objected, Josie always had dinner ready for them. They were surprised when they arrived to find a strange car in the driveway and Randy's pick up truck. "If I didn't know better," Michael said, "I'd bet that was my father's car. Could that be Michelle's surprise? If it is," he lamented, "kiss the weekend goodbye."

Well of course, it was his parents' car. When the crew came in, they were greeted by them, the Fishers, Randy, Lizzie and Michelle. Amidst much confusion, Lizzie found Michael. She jumped into his arms and screeched. "You're going to be my real uncle. Isn't that wonderful?"

Gabby Michael was speechless. He immediately figured out what was going on. He was standing close to his sister, and he asked her, "You and Randy? You're getting married?"

"Tomorrow morning," she said, "and you're all invited."

Michael grabbed her and planted a kiss smack on her forehead. After that, he gave Randy his strongest bear hug, and finally he picked Lizzie up and kissed her tenderly. "It's a privilege to be your real uncle, pumpkin," he said.

At last, he went over to his parents and kissed them. Jerry had already done the honors. His dad admonished him jokingly, "I wondered when you would notice us. Jerry says that he vouches for Randy so I suppose you do to. I pray it's not another mistake."

"I assure you, Dad. Michelle is getting a first rate fellow. They don't come any better. Even before this day, I considered him to be my brother."

All the while, Josie was putting out a big spread for dinner. The food was delicious but Michael was a little upset until his mother told him that the Fishers were so gracious that they were putting them up in Ron's old room. "We can't wait to see the house," his mother added.

"Absolutely, right after the wedding."

When she shopped for the curtains, Michelle had purchased a plain white dress and matching white shoes. Standing next to Randy, as Paul performed the ceremony, she looked angelic. She also looked like a dwarf even though she was 5'9" tall. Lizzie was the flower girl, and looked like a doll in the dress Michelle had bought for her. Warren was Randy's best man, and made a dashing figure in his Sunday best.

Rosie outdid herself, not only with the food, but she had decorated the social hall, and it never looked so festive. While everyone was feeding themselves, Michael's father wanted to meet the man who got Michael and Jerry back into a church. He and Paul had a long chat, and Michael, Sr. was very impressed with him as a minister and as a human being.

"How did you do it?" Michael, Sr. wanted to know.

"There's no magic," Paul said. "I just told them that straight or gay, they had the same worth and love in the eyes of God." They both believed that most ministers don't feel that way. I convinced them that God loves them unconditionally, just like their parents do." Mr. Costello nodded in full agreement.

"Paul," he said, "If it's all right with the Fishers, I'd like to stay until tomorrow and attend your service."

"I'm sure it's all right, but if it isn't, I have a spare bedroom."

Randy, Michelle and Liz took off after the social. They were all going to Disney Land for a few days. The honeymoon was for three. Everyone waved goodbye as they left in Michelle's car, with bells and streamers tied to the back.

The crew took the Costellos to see the house. Of course, they loved it, and wished the boys health and happiness. Then Michael drove them back to the Fishers. He told the Fishers that he had made reservations at Joey's for dinner that evening. Paul, Warren and Dan were joining them. He didn't give them a chance to object.

The Fishers and Costellos became fast friends quickly, and back at the house, the crew made love all afternoon until it was time to shower, dress and head for Joey's. The Fishers were driving the Costellos and Paul, Warren and Dan were coming together.

Driving to Joey's, Jeff became very reflective. His family was growing. His and Jim's business was prospering, and he was getting happier every day. If he had one regret in life, it was that he hadn't recognized his sexual orientation sooner. If he had, he could have avoided his disastrous relationship with Marie. But his bad relationship with Marie made him appreciate his good relationship with Jim all the more.

Joey fussed over Michael's parents, telling them how much he loved Michael and Jerry. He treated the table to lots of freebies. He even sat with them for awhile. At the end of the meal, Michael, Sr. told his son that he wouldn't mind retiring in Lake Henry.

To add to his feeling of 'coming home' he cried all through Paul's inspiring sermon on Sunday. No pastor had ever touched his soul or moved him like Paul did. "No wonder you attend church regularly again," he told his son.

The crew realized that this weekend was a big surprise. It was extra special to all of them, and one they would never forget.

CHAPTER EIGHTEEN

A few days after the wedding, Brian and Tucker were eager to see what the crew had done to their 'hideaway.' They asked their sons for permission to use the place for two or three days during the week with their wives. Jeff called the other members of the crew, who enthusiastically approved.

Jeff warned his fathers that there was plenty of non perishable food at the country home these days, but the Fisher's store was closed for the winter. They needed to supply their own perishables or if there was something special they wanted, they would have to be sure to bring it up with them. The key was no longer under the mat, but they could pick it up at the Fisher's. When the time came, Jeff would call the Fisher's to alert them.

Tuck had a plan. He and Brian arranged to take off three days during the second week of December. Colleen was the chief accountant for a big manufacturing company. Brian knew that Colleen's busiest time was the second week of the month. That was when the corporate books were closed and the monthly financial statements needed to be prepared. Maryann was an assistant principal at a local high school. School was in session and mid term exams were in progress so Tuck knew that Maryann couldn't get away either. Their plan worked well. Both ladies declined to go, but encouraged their husbands to take the much needed time off. They promised to take a drive up to see the place some weekend in the near future. They would all drive up early on a Sunday, and would be able to drive home the same day.

On the Tuesday morning of their trip, Brian and Tuck were as excited as two young school boys. They were on the road by 5:30 AM in Tuck's van. Jeff had told them that the Fishers were expecting them at about eight o'clock. When they arrived, Josie insisted that they have breakfast with them. They could not refuse her offer even though they were anxious to isolate themselves in the country home as soon as possible.

When they arrived at the Fishers, they got a surprise. As long as she was making breakfast, Josie decided to invite a few more friends. She wanted to ask Randy and Michelle, but they had to work. She did invite Dan, Warren and Paul. They all had flexible work schedules and were glad to accept one of Josie's invitations. Brian and Tuck knew that Dan and Warren were a gay couple from talking to their sons. Jerry would not have dreamed of outing Paul, and even Jeff and Jim were still unaware of his sexual preference. Brian and Tuck had no reason to believe he was gay. None of the others believed that Brian and Tuck were anything but straight, either.

Everyone had a good time. They were all very compatible. The Fishers and Warren Jones were about the same age as Brian and Tuck. Dan Harriman and Pastor Paul Patterson were a little younger, but closer in age to their generation, than to the crew's. In no time at all, they were all chatting like old friends. Brian and Tuck noticed that Dan and Warren were not embarrassed to take each others hands once in a while. They smiled inwardly, and lamented at their own closeted situation. They became so lost in all the pleasant banter that they both missed all the signals coming from Paul.

Paul could not tear his eyes away from the two handsomest hunks he had ever seen even though he 'knew' that they were straight. In their maturity, how did they stay so lean and muscular? They had all their hair with only tinges of gray. He kept gazing down at their packages, but they were seated and he couldn't see a thing. Warren and Dan were not so oblivious, and were confused at the sexual tension coming from their pastor. If they ever had a suspicion it was right now.

Finally it was time to go. Brian and Tuck thanked the Fishers for their hospitality and told them they would return the key on Thursday before they left. They shook hands with the others, and when Paul held on a little too long, they both got the first inkling. This prompted Brian to say to him, "Here's my card with my cell phone number. Tuck and I would really like to get to know you better. Any guy who could get Jeff, Jim, and Michael to join his church, and take them away from their catholic upbringing, is someone worth knowing. Not to mention converting Jerry. Call me when you are free and visit with us at the house."

Paul's heart skipped a beat. "Thank you. I'd like that a lot," and he added a hug to his goodbye. He started to leave, but turned around and said, "I'm free this evening. How about I come around about four this afternoon. We can schmooze and then have dinner together."

"That would be great," Tuck told him. "How about going to Joey's Place? My mouth has been watering for his ribs for weeks."

"Sounds like a plan, " Paul answered. He finally, reluctantly left.

Brian and Tuck arrived at the house and could not believe what they saw. The place looked huge. They hurried in and dropped their bags. Then they emptied the car of the perishables and other things they thought they would need. They refrigerated what needed to be refrigerated, and from habit they headed to their usual room. Then they remembered Jeff had told them to use the first room on the right in the new wing. Their old room belonged to Michael and Jerry now. They did as they were instructed. After they put everything away, and made sure the lube could easily be reached from the bed, they stripped and jumped into the bed.

"Listen," Brian said.

"I don't hear anything," Tuck answered.

"Exactly. It's totally silent. No squeaking."

"Yahoo," Tuck yelled as he jumped on top of Brian and began to kiss him passionately. It had been a while since they had enjoyed each other, and they were insatiable. They had eaten a huge breakfast, compliments of Josie Fisher, so lunch wasn't even a consideration. They must have cum three times each before they fell asleep, hugging each other tightly.

They were awakened by the sound of a cell phone playing the William Tell Overture. Brian had to get out of bed to get to his phone. Tuck laughed to himself, he had never seen Brian's cock quite so limp.

"Hello," Brian managed to mumble.

"Hi, it's Paul. I just wanted to give you a heads up, I'll be there in fifteen or twenty minutes."

"Great!" Brian lied, as he hung up. "Come on," he said to Tuck. "Let's try out the new shower. Jeff said that it was big enough for two." They ran the water, but after a few minutes they realized that the water was not getting warm.

"Shit," Tucker yelled. "We forgot to turn on the electricity. I hope we didn't ruin any food. And shit, it's getting cold in here now that the sun is going down." He ran to the utility room which, conveniently could be reached through the bathroom, and he put on the circuit breakers. He noticed that the boys had marked which ones to shut when the house was not used and which ones had to stay on. The furnace was on, so Tuck figured the thermostat needed to be reset. He went into the hallway where he found it and turned it up a few degrees.

In no time the house was toasty warm and the shower was emitting hot water. Brian and Tuck showered together and washed one another where the sun don't shine. They got out of the shower with much reluctance and were drying themselves, when they heard a voice in the living room yelling, "The door was unlocked so I came in."

"We're here in the first bedroom," Brian yelled. "Come on back."

The first thing that Paul thought was, "They're using one bedroom and there are three more available." Once again his heart pumped overtime. Then he entered the bedroom. Brian and Tuck had always had magnificent bodies, and were never shy. They made no attempt to hide their nakedness. There was a chair in the room, and they told Paul to sit. They would be dressed in a jiffy.

"Don't hurry," Paul said laughing. "I'm enjoying the view." He was staring at Brian's still very limp cock. Yet limp as it was, he had never seen one so thick. He wondered how his wife managed. Then he wondered if Tuck managed. Brian and Tuck could never fool a gay man. This caused a little bit of tension in the room, so Tucker said in all seriousness.

"When we used to come down alone in the late spring and early fall, we spent the whole weekend in the nude and went skinny dipping every day. When the weather permits, you are more than welcome to join us in the summer."

"You know, I'd like that," Paul told them. He was sure glad he was seated because his cock was about to rip through his pants. He didn't know that if Brian and Tuck weren't so spent, they would have had to sit down also. They were both dangerously attracted to the minister.

When they were dressed, they all went into the living room. It had gotten a little too cold to sit on the new deck. Brian and Tuck were sad about that. When he stood, Paul's bulging package was obvious, but he decided that he was going to ignore it since it seemed to be out of his control. When they were seated in the living room, Tuck asked if everyone wanted a beer. They all accepted, and he retrieved three cans from the fridge.

Tuck started the conversation. "What have you done to bring so many people flocking to your church? Or maybe I should ask what your philosophy is?"

"It's simple," Paul said. "I can sum it up in a couple of sentences. I believe that Christianity was founded on Christ's principle of unconditional love. That means loving your enemies as well as your neighbors. Nothing gets me angrier than someone who uses the bible and invokes God's name to promote some agenda of hate."

"Do you hate those people?" Brian wanted really to know. He was not goading Paul.

"Absolutely not. They make me angry, just like one of your kids might make you angry, but you still love them. In fact, I pray for those people and send them thoughts of love and healing."

"You are a true messenger of God," Tuck said sincerely. He stood up from his chair and went over and sat next to Paul on the sofa. As soon as he did, he leaned toward the pastor and embraced him. Paul hugged back. When they were finished hugging, Paul's hand inadvertently found itself resting on Tuck's thigh. Brian smiled. This was getting interesting.

"Tell us about you," Brian urged.

"There's not much to tell. After seminary, I drifted from church to church. I kept getting fired because I wouldn't preach fire and brimstone. I lasted only one Sunday at one church because I said in my sermon that everyone was welcome in my church regardless of their race, religion or sexual orientation. That didn't go over well, as you can imagine. I finally got a ministry in St. Paul where my views were accepted. The church grew rapidly, and things were going well for me, but when my spouse died of brain cancer, I resigned. I withdrew from life for a couple of years. When I saw the ad in a church magazine for this position, I was drawn to it. Because the area is so rural, I believed that I could live a quiet, reclusive life. I was interviewed by the Fishers, Dan and Warren, who seemed to embrace my philosophy of Christianity. So here I am."

There was a pause and Tucker said, "Gee, I'm really sorry about your wife."

Paul had made up his mind to come out and he thought to himself why not start with these two great guys, who are obviously a couple. Besides they don't even live here or go to my church.

"There you see. You assumed when I said that I was a widower that my wife died. That's what everybody in town assumed as well, and I was too chicken to correct that assumption. In a sense, I did lose my wife. Patrick was everything to me. I don't know how I survived his loss. I have not ever been with a man since. My fist has been my most loyal lover." Why were Brian and Tuck not totally surprised?

Paul continued. "When I was planning Jerry's baptism, somehow I got up the courage to tell him. I told him that I had decided to come out and be honest with all these people who had taken me into their hearts and made me feel like family. Jerry swore that he wasn't going to tell anyone. That was something I had to do myself. So I'm not making any announcements in the local newspaper or anything like that, but I am coming out as each opportunity occurs. Somehow, and I mean this as a compliment, I felt comfortable telling you guys."

"Wow," Brian sighed.

"And now I want to know all about you guys, and I think you know exactly what I mean," Paul almost made it an ultimatum.

So they took turns relating their story, from their corporate orientation where they shared a room and fell in love, to their decision to live a lie and not shatter the lives of their wives whom they loved dearly. Brian and Tucker were Catholics so they felt like they had just made a confession and they asked Paul to forgive them.

Paul laughed. "I forgive everyone," he said. "It's part of loving unconditionally. If anything is needed, I need to commend you. Your decision to keep your secret and not shatter the lives of the ones you love is truly admirable. You must only forgive yourselves."

By this time Brian and Tucker were sobbing uncontrollably so Paul got up and embraced them both. The three men huddled and hugged one another for a while until Tuck said, "Holy mackerel. Look at the time. We'd better get going." They disentangled and Paul said, "I'll drive. I'm blocking your car."

When they arrived at Joey's Place, Joey greeted them all warmly, with a hug for all three. They all ordered a full rack of ribs. The waiter served four or five sides family style, Brian and Tucker had not had lunch in favor of having sex so they were truly starved. Paul had a pretty good appetite too. After coming out to Brian and Tuck, he felt as if a burden had been released from his shoulders, and it translated into a very healthy appetite. Not only that but he felt so comfortable with them, and he was so happy with the fact that he could at last be himself, without any cover ups, after so long a time.

As they approached the end of the meal, they realized that they were the only customers left in the restaurant. Joey happened to pass by and told them not to rush. The restaurant was officially open for another hour. They had a table in a far corner, and they could speak freely without fear of being overheard. Brian and Tucker were sitting on each side of Paul.

Brian smiled at Tucker and asked, "Are you thinking what I'm thinking?"

"I'm pretty sure," Tuck answered.

They both reached under the table and put a hand on each of Paul's knees. Paul was happily surprised and made no move to remove the hands. Tuck hesitated for just a moment, took a deep breath, and then said to Paul.

"We, Brian and I, believe you have been celibate too long. We were wondering if you would like to spend the night with us tonight."

Paul answered them by breaking into tears. "I can't imagine a better ending to a perfect evening," he said. And then he sobbed some more.

Now they were all of the same mind to finish up and get home quickly. They started to leave, when Joey sat down at the fourth place at the table. It seemed that he had time now to sit and socialize. They all started to make small talk when suddenly Brian yawned.

"Gee, I'm sorry," he said. Tuck and I have been up since 5 AM and I'm bushed. Will you excuse us please Joey. I need to get some shut eye." And so they were able to leave the restaurant.

Paul pulled up in front of the house in back of Tuck's van. As they got into the house, he was visibly shaking. He seemed a wee bit frightened. Brian put his arms around him and kissed him lightly on the lips. "It's OK," he quipped. "We promise to be gentle." That got Paul laughing and he relaxed. He followed them expectantly into their bedroom.

Brian and Tuck undressed quickly, but Paul seemed to take forever so they started to remove the rest of his clothing for him. He loved what they were doing and he let them continue to undress him. As they removed his clothing their fingers played mischievously across his body. They left him in his boxer shorts. Then Tuck fell to his knees and pulled down Paul's boxers. Paul's cock jumped up and hit Tuck in the nose. Everyone howled and began to laugh uncontrollably, until Tuck grabbed Paul's cock and started to suck it. Paul exchanged his laughter for a sigh and a deep moan of contentment. Brian began to kiss Paul. His tongue forced Paul's lips apart and their tongues engaged.

"Would you like to fuck me?" Brian asked him "or do you want to be fucked?"

With no hesitation, Paul answered, "Both!"

Tuck stopped sucking and said, "I really hoped you'd say that." Brian's too big for your almost virgin ass, so you fuck him and I'll fuck you. It was amazing that there was absolutely no reticence between them. To hold back was to do them all a disservice.

Brian lay down flat on his back and lifted his legs to his chest. Tuck took the lube and filled Brian's love hole and then he put plenty on Paul's cock. Paul began to moan, "Oh Tuck that feels so good. It's been too long." Tuck got a tear in his eye and gave Paul a sloppy wet kiss on his buttocks. Paul positioned himself at the entrance to Brian's crack and Tuck guided him in. Paul was thinner than Tuck and he slid easily into Brian's well trained ass.

"Don't move, "Tuck instructed Paul. He bent down and began to rim Paul's crack. Paul was beginning to think that God had called him home this very night. Before he could swoon dead away, Tuck generously lubed Paul's ass. He had no idea if Paul would be able to take him right away or if he would have to loosen him up first. He easily inserted his middle finger into Paul, and without meaning to, he grazed Paul's prostate. Paul spasmed with pleasure and almost fell out of Brian, but he pushed right back in. Tuck inserted another finger and a third and still Paul took it easily. He guessed that Patrick had been very fat in the cock like Brian, and Paul had remained stretched even after all these years. He took his fingers out and entered Paul's greedy ass. Nobody moved. They just lay still, each lost in his own thoughts, enjoying the thrill of a three way with people they loved. Finally Paul moaned, "Oh guys, I can't tell you how great this feels. Thank you so much.'

"No need for thanks," Tuck said, "We're enjoying this just as much as you are." That said, he started to pump in and out of Paul, who then did the same to Brian. Needless to say, Paul had been celibate so long, he came much too soon. But by the same token he recovered quickly and never fell out of Brian. Tuck and Paul fell into a steady rhythm, and Brian joined the dance by thrusting upward as Paul thrust down.

Poor Paul was not expecting the kind of noise Brian and Tuck made when they came. As they got closer and closer their moaning, groaning and screaming got louder. If he didn't know what was going on, and if he was in another room, Paul would have thought that they were being murdered. Paul's cock was treating Brian's prostate to unbearable ecstasy, and he came with one of the loudest screams Tuck had ever heard. As he did so his ass squeezed tight around Paul's cock and Paul came with tears in his eyes and a lot quieter than Brian. Now it was Paul's turn to squeeze his asshole involuntarily and that triggered Tuck's orgasm.

They lay in a heap, all tangled up, reluctant to disengage, but eventually they did. Paul began to cry like a baby. Brian kissed the tears off one eye and Tuck kissed the tears off the other. Finally Tuck got a towel to wipe away

Brian's cum. He turned out the light in the bedroom and the three of them fell asleep, crunched together on a queen size mattress.

CHAPTER NINETEEN

The crew arrived at their country home late one wintry Friday evening. Someone asked if he should turn on the television and the others all groaned, "No."

"You know what I'd like to do?" Michael asked. The others looked at him waiting to hear what he had in mind. "I'd like to take a shower with my guy and then fuck him 'til he cries for mercy."

"Sounds good to me," Jerry smiled at Michael.

"Gives me a couple of ideas or three," Jim said.

"Me too," Ron echoed.

"I've got a great idea," Foster said. "It's sort of a variation on a theme. How about we put our names in a bowl and we each draw a name out. If you get your partner you have to throw it back. Whoever you draw is yours for the night. You shower with that guy, suck him; fuck him or whatever the two of you decide to do. And you sleep with him all night also."

"Fantastic idea," Michael said.

They had debated getting a land phone, but in the end they decided they should. There was a pad and pencil near the phone in the kitchen. Michael took a sheet from the pad and tore it into three pieces. On each one he wrote the name of one member of a partnership, and folded the pieces of scrap paper.

He found a deep bowl and put the papers inside. Then he lined up the other members of the partnership and asked them to draw a name. They had to do it four times before nobody drew his own partner's name. In the end it was Jim and Foster, Jeff and Jerry, Michael and Ron.

Jim grabbed Foster's hand. "Let's claim the big shower before someone else does," he said.

"I don't mind the small shower at all," Jeff said. He grabbed Jerry and headed to the old shower.

"I guess we'll wait it out," Michael said. He looked at Ron. "By the way," he asked Ron, "your place or mine?" He took Ron in his arms and began to kiss him gently while fondling Ron's package.

Ron murmured into Michael's ear, "This is going to be a fantastic night."

It was. During the night the snow fall measured about eighteen inches. The crew was indeed snowed in. They played all night, and after breakfast they took back their own partners and played all day. By the middle of the afternoon the snow plows had done their work, and the blinding sun had begun to melt most of what remained. By Sunday, the crew was able to start for home about 7 PM, after another fantastic meal prepared by Ron's mom.

On Monday morning about 10 AM, Pastor Paul received a phone call from Brian O'Toole. When he picked up the phone and the caller identified himself, Paul's pants immediately tented.

"How nice to hear your voice," he said. "I sure miss you guys."

"We miss you too," Brian answered him. "Listen buddy, we have a proposition for you and it's one we hope you won't refuse. Tomorrow morning Tuck and I are driving up to Flagstaff. We have a client there that is having some problems we hope to resolve. We expect to be there until Friday afternoon. As you know, Lake Henry is on our way. If you could get away for a few days, we could pick you up on our way to Flagstaff and drop you off on our way home. We promise you we'll have a fantastic time there."

"Wow," Paul gasped. "That is fantastic. I've been here over three years and have not had a vacation. I'm sure it can be arranged. Let me speak to Warren Jones. He's head of our church board. I'll clear it with him, and call you back."

"Great," Brian said. "Just give us an answer by tonight. Do you have my cell number? It would be best to call on that phone." Paul didn't have it so Brian gave it to him and Paul repeated it twice so he wouldn't screw up.

As soon as he got off the phone, Paul made a momentous decision. This was his opportunity to come out. He called Warren and asked him if he would please come over to the church today as early as possible.

"Is it church business?" Warren wanted to know.

"In a sort of way," Paul hedged.

"I'm on my way. Have the coffee ready," Warren laughed.

When Warren arrived, Paul took him into his office where he had a little hot plate on which he was brewing coffee. He also had a tiny fridge with milk, butter and some bagels inside. He purposely wasted time, serving and setting everything up, because frankly he was nervous.

When he could delay no longer he began. "Warren, dear friend, I need to apologize to the whole congregation, but especially to you. I didn't exactly lie to you, but I let you believe something that wasn't true."

Warren opened his mouth to speak but Paul asked him to kindly remain silent until he finished or he would lose his nerve. Warren complied.

Paul also had decided to modify his story slightly, not because he wanted to continue with any lies, but to protect the identity of Brian and Tucker. If Warren knew who he was going away with, they would be outed. He continued.

"When I was being interviewed, I indicated that I was a widower. This is absolutely true. You all assumed that I had lost a wife. The truth is I lost my spouse, my best friend, my lover. His name was Patrick. He died of a brain tumor."

Warren wanted desperately to speak, but held his tongue as Paul had requested.

"I should have corrected the misconception, but I honestly believed that I could never again be with another man so what would it matter? So I let it be. Now it matters. I recently met someone, and let's say we got very close to each other. He's not in any position to commit to me, and that's OK, but Warren, he's the first man I have been with in nearly four years. I have an extraordinary opportunity to be with him from tomorrow to Friday, so I'd like the time off."

"Paul, you oaf," Warren chided. "Of course you can take the time off. You have never had a day off since you have been here. But let me tell you a couple of things and you listen until I'm finished before you say anything. First of all, you know the old adage, 'it takes one to know one'? Well, Dan and I have never had a doubt that you were gay, but we needed for you to tell us. As for the rest of the congregation, they probably have an inkling, but I don't think you have to come out ever, unless you want to set up housekeeping with some lucky guy. As for who you are going away with, it's a 'they' not a 'he,' isn't it?"

"How in the world..." Paul started to say but was speechless.

"We saw how they looked at each other, how they looked at you, how you looked at them. Why, Dan and I have been kicking the possibility around for some time now. I guess you were trying to keep from outing them, and I can respect that. So here's what I propose just so we can continue to protect their privacy. I'll tell everyone that you are going on a retreat. Tomorrow morning bring your car over to my house. We can park it in the rear and nobody will see it. Then tell Brian and Tuck to pick you up at my place. Tell them it will be all right to come in to get you. Their secret is safe with us. I'll have hot coffee ready for them. Feel better?"

Paul answered by breaking into tears.

"Oh man, don't do that. I just fall apart when a man cries," Warren said. He took Paul in his arms, hugged him tightly and surprised Paul by kissing him on the lips.

"Where are you guys going?" he finally remembered to ask.

"They have business in Flagstaff. That's where we'll be."

"Better dress warm, Warren suggested. "It gets mighty cold up there."

"I think I'll be warm enough," Paul smiled at Warren and Warren started to laugh hysterically. He hugged and kissed Paul one more time, and as he left Paul said, "I'll let you know later what time I'll be at your place. I only know that it will be early."

Immediately Warren was out the door, Paul called Brian. The first thing he asked was if Brian was alone and could he talk for a few minutes. Brian gave him the go ahead and Paul explained everything that had transpired between Warren and him. Brian was incredulous. "Can't we hide our love from anyone?" he asked, more to himself than to Paul.

"Not to a gay person, it seems." Then Paul gave Brian detailed instructions how to get to Warren and Dan. He asked what time they would get there, and advised that they leave time for coffee and something with Dan and Warren. Warren insisted and Paul said that it was the least they could do.

"We're leaving early and should be there by 8 AM," Brian announced, and they ended the conversation. Paul hung up and had to catch his breath. He was literally hyperventilating. Life had not been this exciting for him in many years. He opened one of his dresser drawers and beneath some underwear and socks there was a picture album. He took out the album, sat on his bed and opened it. The album contained close to twenty years of beautiful memories.

He turned to the first page and there was a picture of his Patrick on the day they had met. It had been taken at a country fair. Beautiful Patrick, so kind, so sweet, so full of love. Paul began to cry as he ran his finger tips over the picture.

He was young then, in his early twenties, just out of the seminary. There was a carnival in town, and having nothing better to do he went to the fair, if for nothing else, a good hot dog. Wandering down the fairway, he decided to have a go at the ring toss. He bought three tosses and each time he tossed, he missed badly. He was about to walk away when he heard a voice say to him, "You're doing it all wrong. Here let me show you." He turned to see a handsome young man in his mid twenties who had come up beside him and had purchased three tosses.

"You're not following through," he said. "As soon as the ring leaves your hand, you stop you're forward motion. Look," he said. He tossed a ring and followed through so that his arm nearly went straight out and forward. The ring landed on the bottle neck and fell onto it. He had two more successes and won a prize.

"What would you like," he asked Paul. Paul looked at the prizes. There was nothing he really wanted but the stranger was serious and he was afraid the man would be insulted if he didn't accept.

"OK. I'll take the Betty Boop doll," he said laughing.

The vendor handed him the doll, and the stranger extended his hand. "I'm Patrick Mackey," he said pumping Paul's hand.

"Paul Patterson here," Paul answered unable to take his eyes off Patrick. God, he was gorgeous. Paul's heart beat was accelerating.

"I'm new in town," Patrick said. I don't know a soul." Could I interest you in sharing a hot dog with me?"

"That's what I came here for. But I'm paying. It's the least I can do for my Betty Boop doll." He laughed as he said it. They walked together until they found a hot dog stand. They each ordered it with mustard and sauerkraut. Paul also paid for two cokes. They found a bench and sat down to have their dogs.

"So what brings you to town?" Paul asked Patrick.

"I've just been hired to manage the new shoe factory on Regal Street," he answered. "And what do you do?"

"I'm the brand new pastor at the Faith Ministry Church on Front Street. I hope that won't scare you away," Paul joked.

"Not on your life, Pastor

Remembering those first precious moments, Paul began to sob bitterly. He looked at Patrick's picture and said, "My darling Patrick, please approve of what I am doing with Brian and Tucker. They are really good men."

Paul almost fell off the bed. He distinctly heard Patrick's voice saying, "Of course I approve baby. I arranged for you to meet them. Not only that, but through them, you'll meet the one to spend the rest of your life with. Just trust me." Then Paul rationalized. What a vivid imagination I've got.

Brian and Tucker were at Warren's and Dan's at the appointed time. As they parked in the driveway, they couldn't see Paul's car and assumed he wasn't there yet. That was a good thing. Paul's car was parked in the rear of the house, away from prying eyes.

They knocked on the front door and a smiling Dan Harriman answered. As soon as they were inside and the door was closed behind them, Dan greeted Brian and Tuck with a bone crushing hug. "Thank you for making Paul so happy," he said. They could smell fresh coffee brewing in the kitchen and headed for the smell.

Warren and Paul were setting the kitchen table with cups and saucers, butter and jam, milk and a tray full of assorted bagels. They interrupted to greet Brian and Tuck with hugs and kisses. Brian thought, "When we were totally in the closet, we were never greeted this way. It's what we missed all these years. Thank God, there are people we can trust with our secret now."

They spent about an hour with Warren and Dan and then headed for Flagstaff. The closer they got, the more snow was at the side of the highway, but the roads were clear. They found the motel the firm had booked for them. It was in the heart of the business district and if they wanted to, Brian and Tuck could walk to their client. Brian went in alone to check them in. Tuck and Paul stayed in the car. The man at the desk was in his late thirties and cute as the dickens. Brian asked him if he could give them a room away from traffic for maximum quiet and privacy. The desk clerk smiled at the handsome man in front of him and gave him a corner room at the end of the hall so there would be little traffic. He noticed that the reservation was for two. From his position at the desk he could see the car parked out in front. There were definitely two men seated in the car. He said nothing, but smiled inwardly. He instructed Brian to drive to the far end of the motel and around the back so as to be parked as close as possible to the assigned room.

When Brian opened the door he was pleased to see two queen size beds. "Perfect," he said. The men hung up their clothes and filled the drawers with socks, underwear and shirts. It was just after noon. Tuck suggested that they have lunch at the hotel, and then he and Brian would visit their client for a couple of hours.

"You can warm up the bed for us," Tucker suggested to Paul.

Actually he did. All three men had gotten up very early that morning. Paul had been too excited to sleep and was up most of the night, so as soon as Brian and Tuck left, he took a nice long, very hot shower and fell into one of the beds in the nude. He fell asleep instantly on top of the bed cover. He didn't even wake up when Brian and Tuck opened the door and saw him lying there. Paul's nude body was a beautiful sight and Brian and Tuck were filled with lust. They undressed as quietly as possible and then from each side of the bed they leaned into Paul's sleeping torso and began to lick his cock. In an instant Paul was erect, and Brian could easily work on his cock head which had shot out of his foreskin, and Tuck could work on his shaft.

Paul woke moaning loudly and with each hand he pushed Brian and Tuck further into him. They stopped sucking and got into bed on each side of Paul. They all snuggled as best they could. They kissed each other with open mouths and darting tongues all the while groping someone else's cock.

Suddenly Brian said, "The first time we made love (Paul noted that Brian said 'made love' not 'had sex') Paul had the privilege of being in the middle. This time I want that honor."

Tuck and Paul nodded their heads in assent and Tuck said, "Don't worry, love, we'll all have a chance in the middle before we head for home on Friday.

The three then positioned themselves so Brian was in the middle. They fucked until they all came in furious spurts and loud shrieking yells. They made so much noise they had to laugh at themselves. After a brief rest they repositioned themselves so that Tuck was the middleman and they repeated their performances until they came again. They lay spent for quite a while until Tuck said, "I don't know about you guys but I'm starved."

Reluctantly they got out of bed. All three squeezed into the shower and made sure that all the tell tale evidence of their love making was washed away. They dressed warmly for the cold night. There was a spritz of snow in the air. When they got to the front desk, the cute guy was not there, but a pleasant young woman was at the desk. They asked her to recommend a nearby restaurant where they could have dinner. She told them that there was a very nice restaurant just around the corner. It wasn't fancy or expensive but they would get a hearty, tasty dinner. When she told them that the name of the place was Joey's Café, they all laughed. She looked at them strangely and Paul told her that it was an inside joke.

The woman was correct. The food was ample, tasty and inexpensive. They all ordered steaks. Paul had mashed potatoes and Brian and Tuck, who worked out constantly, bravely ordered French fries. They had coffee and apple pie for dessert. They asked their waiter about breakfast, but he said they were only open for lunch and dinner. The motel coffee shop would have to do.

When they got back they all snuggled into one bed. Paul was in the middle. Suddenly he sat up and leaned over. He sucked Brian's cock for a while, much to Brian's delight and then he leaned the other way and obliged Tuck, who was equally as delighted. They were pretty well spent so after a while, they all fell asleep even though they were a jumble of intertwined arms and legs.

In the morning they used the bathroom one at a time. They all liked their privacy for at least part of the morning routine. While one of them was in the bathroom, the other two played sixty nine. The only one who came again that morning was Paul. Poor guy! He had been denied for so long.

After they dressed they went to the motel coffee shop and ordered three different meals. Paul had French toast; Brian had pancakes; Tuck had eggs over with bacon and a bagel. They all had coffee, regular. None of them used milk or sugar. After breakfast, they checked the weather. It was still overcast and there were snow flurries in the air so Brian and Tuck decided to drive to their client a few blocks away. They hated to leave Paul alone and without transportation, but Paul said he didn't mind at all.

Paul watched TV in the room for an hour or so. After a while, he got bored with that and walked down to the lobby. They always had brochures for tourist attractions. Often the bus to an attraction picked you up at your motel. Then again they were in a down town location. Maybe there was something to see or do right near the motel.

When he walked into the hotel lobby, he saw the desk clerk who Brian thought was so cute. He had to agree. The clerk was maybe a couple of years younger than he was. He was about the same height, 6'1". His eyes were blue. He had brown curly hair, and Paul was very attracted to him.

"Hi," Paul said. "I was wondering if you could recommend any sights of interest in the immediate area. I have no transportation, but I'd like to get out a little."

"There's an art museum a couple of blocks up the street, but it won't be open until 12 PM. Aside from that there's really nothing else," the handsome man informed him. It's pretty quiet at this desk too. Why don't you hang out with me in the lobby and we can chat some." Paul thought that was a pretty good idea.

He extended his hand and introduced himself merely as Paul. The desk clerk took Paul's hand and said, "Nice to meet you Paul. I'm Doug."

Doug would never know what prompted his next question. It was almost as if he was being cued by an off stage prompter. "You're staying with that couple, Mr. Simmons and Mr. O'Toole aren't you?" he asked.

"Why yes," Paul answered. How did you know?"

"I saw you in the car with Mr. Simmons when Mr. O'Toole was checking you guys in. He checked two people in and there were obviously three of you and two beds. It doesn't take much imagination," he said.

"You're being very presumptuous," Paul said. But he said it with a smile on his face and that let Doug know that it was OK if he figured it out.

"You don't have to worry about me. It's perfectly all right if you want to be a threesome. It's just that I'm very jealous. I don't get much action in this part of the world." Doug motioned Paul to sit down on a sofa in the lobby. He came around from behind the desk and joined Paul on the sofa.

"Why do you stay here then?" Paul wanted to know.

"My folks died when I was in college. I had four younger brothers and sisters ranging in age from two to fourteen. I had to quit college and go to work to support them. The two oldest made it through college on scholarships and they helped me a little with the two youngest. Ricky and Donny are just not college material but they are grown now and on their own. Actually I have been looking for work that will pay me some real money, not what I earn here. Also I'd like to get away from here. There are too many bad memories."

"What kind of work are you looking for?" Paul asked.

"Well, I became a whiz at building and repairing homes. I had no money to maintain our house so I had to do it all my own. I can do it all, from carpentry to plumbing and wiring."

"Have you ever heard of Lake Henry?" Paul asked. Doug shook his head, indicating that he had not. Paul continued. "It's between here and Phoenix only closer to Phoenix. It's pretty rural and there's not much excitement. The younger people go into Phoenix on the weekends if they want to sow some wild oats. But it's the friendliest community that I have ever lived in, and that includes gay friendly." Paul winked at Doug, who smiled back and patted Paul's hand, sending electricity coursing up his spine.

"I have a friend there that owns his own construction company. I could call him and see if he needs help, if you're interested that is. I don't want to railroad you."

"Do you live there?" Doug asked and Paul nodded yes. "Then I'm interested." They smiled at each other and this time Paul could not help but put his hand on Doug's. Paul took out his cell phone and dialed Randy. There was no answer, but just as he was about to hang up, Randy came on the line.

"Hi Randy," he said "Paul here. I'm in Flagstaff. I was wondering if you need any additional workers."

"Are you kidding me? I am so short handed I could use three guys right now. Why are you asking?" Paul filled him in on his conversation with Doug, and Randy asked to speak with Doug. Doug nervously took the phone and began a phone interview with Randy. Paul could hear only Doug's part of the conversation, but it was obvious that the interview was going well. Doug was fairly beaming.

Then Paul heard Doug tell Randy that he would give notice today, and as soon as he could arrange to move he would be down to Lake Henry. Then he started to laugh just before he hung up. "That's incredible," Doug said. "My last name is Jones also."

He turned to Paul, when he finished his conversation with Randy and hugged him so hard, Paul lost his breath and gained an erection.

"It's not going to take long for me to get out of here. I sold the house when my kid brothers moved out and I rent a furnished room in a boarding house. I have some clothes and my tools, and nothing to hold me back. Will you help me get a place to stay when I get there?"

"I've got an extra bedroom and I live alone, if that would suit you," Paul prayed that it would.

"I'd pay you for my food and lodgings," Doug told Paul. He wanted it to be quite clear that he was not a free loader.

"Of course!" Paul reassured him. Doug grabbed Paul and hugged him once again. All the while Paul had been listening to Randy and Doug interviewing each other, a thought was going through his mind. He decided to spring it on Doug right now.

"Do you think you could be ready to leave by Friday afternoon?" he asked, and Doug nodded yes. "Well if you really don't have much stuff, you could come back in the van with my friends and me."

"OMG! How can I thank you enough?" Doug's shoulders started to shake and he was working hard to hold back tears. Paul wrapped his arms around Doug and held him tight.

"Don't cry, my friend. Something tells me that a brand new life is starting for both of us."

At that moment Paul clearly heard Patrick's voice saying, "See I told you there was a reason I sent Brian and Tucker to you."

Doug pulled out of Paul's grip. "Did you hear that?" he asked Paul. "I distinctly heard someone's voice." Before Paul could begin to register shock, the phone rang and Doug ran to answer it.

When the call was over he said to Paul, "I close the desk for an hour between noon and 1 PM. Would you please have lunch with me, on me?" Prompted by Patrick whispering in his brain, and almost like an automaton Paul said, "Buy me a sandwich or something, and we'll have lunch in my room."

"That's an offer I can't refuse," Doug answered him. He closed the desk and engaged the answering machine at 11:30. He took his lunch box from under the desk, and they went to the coffee shop. Paul asked for a tuna fish salad sandwich and a coke. Then they rushed back to Paul's room. Housekeeping had not yet made up the room so Doug put a 'Do Not Disturb' sign on the door. They double locked the door and fell into each other's arms.

Doug hadn't been with anyone in ages and he came repeatedly. To his credit, Paul who had sex all night kept up with him. Finally Doug washed up and headed back to the lobby. It was almost 2 PM, but there was only one message from his angry manager. Doug called back and gave notice saying he was leaving Friday after lunch. The manager called him a fucker and told him to finish his shift and not come back tomorrow. He would cover the desk himself until he found someone.

Paul sat with Doug all afternoon until he was relieved by the pleasant lady who had told them where to eat. He and Doug sat in the lobby until Brian and Tucker came in. Before they could say anything or show surprise, Paul asked if they would drive Doug and him to Doug's boarding house so he could get his stuff and bring it back to the motel with him. He said he would explain everything on the way to the boarding house. In the car Paul and Doug began their narrative, and all Brian and Tucker could say, when Paul and Doug stopped for breath occasionally, was, "WOW!"

While Doug was putting his meager belongings into a beat up suit case, Paul said to Brian and Tuck that when they got back to the motel, he would take another room.

"When did you get shy?" Brian asked. "We have one whole queen size bed that's going to waste. Don't you think it would be fun watching us make love and vice versa?"

"I'll have to clear that with Doug," Paul answered. Doug was even more starved for love and affection than Paul had been and he thought that it was a capital idea. For the rest of this trip, Paul was certainly not bored and he had plenty to do while Brian and Tuck were at work.

It occurred to Paul that if Doug was going to stay with him at home, he didn't want people thinking he was just a boarder. He determined to come out to everyone who didn't know yet, so he could be honest about his relationship.

When they got Doug settled in the room, Tuck said that he wanted to celebrate and asked Doug to recommend a really good restaurant and not worry about the cost. Doug said it wasn't necessary, but Tuck insisted. They ended up at a country club whose dining room was open to the public. Fortunately Doug was still wearing his work clothes, which included a tie and jacket, as were Brian and Tuck. Paul had to put on a tie and jacket which were supplied by the restaurant.

Doug had been so overwhelmed by the events of the day that during dinner he finally got around to asking Paul what he did for a living. When Paul told him that he was the pastor of the only church in Lake Henry, the look on Doug's face was so precious that they all broke out laughing.

That night as they all got ready for bed and everyone was naked, nobody, not even Doug, was self conscious. Paul and Doug heard the sounds of love coming from Brian's and Tuck's bed. They couldn't help but turn to look. Brian and Tuck were in a sixty-nine position, happily lost in their rapture. Doug whispered in Paul's ear. "Oral sex this afternoon was fantastic, but it's been so long since I've been with anyone. Please fuck me. I need to feel you inside of me."

Paul was happy to oblige. There was a tube of lube on the night table between the two beds. He put Doug on his back and placed a pillow beneath his ass. He lubed Doug's ass well, first with one finger and then with two. There was no resistance so he then lubed his own cock, placed it at Doug's crack and started to enter slowly. All Doug could do was to repeat over and over "Oh God, oh God" until Paul had gone as far as he could go.

"Fuck me hard," Doug begged, and Paul began stroking slowly and sensuously. As both their passions increased, Paul stroked harder and faster. Suddenly Paul felt something at his own crack. A very stiff lubricated prick was poking at his asshole. He reached back to help guide the cock in and he knew it was Tuck. Brian was twice as fat. In the meantime Brian had leaned over Doug and was brushing Doug's lips with his cock. Doug encircled Brian's cock with his fist and guided it into his hungry mouth. The four hot studs all came within seconds of each other.

"You see," Tuck announced, "I keep telling those young kids it doesn't fall off over forty." Everyone laughed.

They fell asleep in a tangle. Brian was the first to wake. He laughed to himself because he was sharing a bed with Paul and Doug. Tuck was alone in the other bed. He got out of bed as quietly as possible and joined Tuck. They hunkered together and Brian fell asleep again, wrapped up in Tuck's warm and inviting arms.

After Brian and Tuck showered and went off to work, Doug put the 'Do Not Disturb" sign on the door and got back in bed with Paul. Two hours later they removed the sign, showered, dressed, and went down for some breakfast. The maid entered the room almost immediately.

At breakfast Paul remembered to tell Doug one important thing. He explained that Brian and Tuck were married to women, and he was to preserve their secret. Everyone who knew about them was determined to preserve their secret romance.

A Boner Book

CHAPTER TWENTY

On Friday morning, Brian and Tuck got up very early. They showered and got ready for work. They packed their suitcases including all their toiletries. Paul and Doug were awake but reluctant to get out of bed.

Tuck said, "It's a beautiful day guys. We're going to have breakfast and then walk to our client. We should be there for about two hours. Please get yourselves ready to start back for home. I'm leaving the car keys on the dresser. Pack the car, make sure the room is cleared out and we'll meet you in the lobby in about two and a half hours. As soon as we check out, we'll be on our way."

The moment Brian and Tuck left, Paul and Doug rolled toward each other and started kissing. Their morning woodies ground hard against each other. Paul pulled away. "We'll have a lifetime together, my dear friend. Next time we make love, let it be in 'our' bed in 'our' house." Doug smiled but his eyes filled with tears. He took Paul's hand and they went to shower together.

After they packed the car and made sure nothing had been left in the room, they went to the coffee shop in the hotel. They took their time and lingered in the shop until Paul felt that Brian and Tuck would be arriving any minute. They took a seat on the sofa in the lobby where they had first talked and fallen in love. It was uncomfortable for Doug because his ex-boss was behind the counter. He was the very same manager who had called Doug a fucker.

After a few uncomfortable minutes, Larry, the manager, called Doug over to the desk. He extended his hand to Doug and said, 'Look Doug, I'm sorry for what I said. I was just so upset at losing such a good worker. To tell the truth, I knew it was bound to happen. You're just way too good for this job." Then he reached under the desk and found an envelope which he gave to Doug. "I was afraid I wouldn't see you, and if you didn't contact me after what I said, I wouldn't know where to send your final pay and your W-2 at the end of the year. Anyhow, here's your final pay check."

"Gee thanks," Doug said. "Actually I am so excited about my new job I forgot all about it. I swear, Larry, it happened so suddenly, I just couldn't give you more notice." He called Paul over and asked Paul to please give the manager his home address and telephone number so he could forward his mail. Paul was thrilled to do it and Larry thanked them both. He was shaking Doug's hand and wishing him well when Brian and Tuck came in.

"Tuck said, "I see the car is right out front ready to go so let's get this show on the road." He settled the bill with his company credit card and then they piled in the van and headed to Lake Henry.

"What time do you estimate we'll get home?" Paul asked Tuck who was driving.

"Well, with a stop for lunch and a couple of pit stops, I figure between 4:30 and 5 PM. Why do you ask?"

"I want to make sure Dan and Warren are home when you drop us off. I want them to be the first to meet Doug, and I need their advice on how to handle my coming out party. I also think that we should celebrate tonight at our favorite celebration spot, Joey's." Then he added, "It's my treat, of course. You guys should have dinner before you head back to Phoenix any way." Brian and Tuck agreed immediately.

Paul called Dan on his cell phone. He asked if he and Warren could be home by 4:30 and asked him to make a reservation for six at 5:30 at Joey's. He told Dan he would explain when they got there.

Then Brian and Tucker left messages for their wives, who were at work, to expect them home about 9:30 PM, give or take a half hour.

The van pulled up at Dan's and Warren's at about 4:40 PM. Dan and Warren were looking for them and came out to greet them. Everybody helped transfer Paul's and Doug's gear to Paul's car, and then went inside.

Dan spoke first. "Who's this hunk here, Paul? And just what are we celebrating."

"This specimen of perfect manhood is Douglas Jones. I've already established no relationship, Warren." Then he pointed at Dan and Warren and introduced them to Doug. They all sat down in the living room and Paul related the story about how they met and how desperately Doug needed to start a new life away from Flagstaff. He told about his call to Randy and the fact that Doug was going to start working for Randy on Monday morning. He explained to Doug that Warren was Randy's uncle. He told Warren and Dan that he was going to take Doug over to Randy's tomorrow to meet him.

Warren got up and went to the fridge. He took out a big bottle of champagne as Dan went for some fluted drinking glasses. "I figured that if we were going to Joey's you might have something to celebrate so I thought why not start the celebration right here." Dan poured the champagne and everyone drank to Paul and Doug, who broke into tears. They all hugged and kissed the newly united couple and urged them to stow the tears. After all, this is a celebration not a funeral.

As they piled into Tuck's van and started out for Joey's Place, Jeff's van was just pulling up in front of the Fishers. This weekend, as usual, Josie wouldn't take no for an answer. She had already made dinner for all of them, "before they holed themselves up in their house for the weekend." Those were her very words.

After dinner at Joey's, Tucker dropped his passengers off at Dan's and Warren's, and he and Brian headed for Phoenix. Paul told Dan and Warren that he wanted to discuss something with them before he and Doug went home. They all gathered in the living room again. Warren asked if anybody wanted an after dinner drink or coffee or something, and everyone declined.

Paul started, "I need to tell my congregants that Doug and I are life partners but I just don't know how to do it. Any advice?" he asked.

Warren spoke first. "Yeah, keep it simple. After the service, Doug, when Paul goes to the back of the church to greet the people as they either go home or to the social hall, you stand beside him. That will give him the opportunity to introduce you and tell them who you are."

"I agree," Dan said, but I would do one more thing. Paul, when you ask everyone to join in the social hour, why don't you announce that you are today's sponsor in honor of your new union with Doug. I'll bet everyone will come to the social hall after that statement. Remember you said a few weeks ago that Jerry was sponsoring the social in honor of his baptism."

Everyone agreed that their plan was the way to go. Doug looked very uncomfortable. He was beginning to think he had lost a little control of his life and the best thing to do was to just ride the crest of the wave until he reached solid ground again.

At long last, Paul and Doug reached Paul's house. Doug was trembling as they approached the front door, and Paul was crying. "If you weren't heavier than I, and if our arms weren't full of suitcases and tools, I'd carry you over the threshold," Paul quipped.

"Even if you don't," Doug told Paul, "I won't mind a bit if you demand your spousal rights."

"Fear not. I will."

When he entered his house, Paul felt overwhelmed and nearly swooned. "What's wrong, Paul?" Doug needed to know.

"Nothing, nothing is wrong. I was just thinking how lonely this place has been for three years and now it's just become my Garden of Eden. I'm just so full of emotion."

Doug grabbed Paul in his arms and started to laugh. "Funny, I don't look like Eve," he joked, and he covered Paul's lips with his.

They put Doug's tools in a storage shed in the back yard, and then went in to the master bedroom to make room for Doug's clothes. The closet was big enough to house Paul's meager wardrobe, and Doug's even more meager one, with room to spare. The same went for the dresser drawers. Paul actually had two drawers that were empty and easily took Doug's socks, underwear and a few shirts. Paul thought that both of them probably should buy some new clothes.

When they were totally settled in, they sat together on the sofa in the living room to watch the evening news. Unfortunately, it became impossible to watch TV. They began making out, kissing, smooching, groping and just hugging one another. So they secured the house for the night, showered together and crawled into Paul's bed, make that, their bed.

"Please fuck me," Doug begged.

"Only if you fuck me first," Paul answered as he dove down on Doug's cock and started sucking at it wildly. As he did, he distinctly felt Patrick's kiss on his cheek and he heard Patrick say, "I love you."

Doug heard Patrick also, and thinking it was Paul, he said, "I love you too."

As Doug and Paul were beginning their first night together alone and as a couple, the crew was unlocking the front door of their house. Almost everything they needed for the weekend was always kept in the house now. The Fishers would not be opening the store for a few more weeks so they did bring some provisions which they brought in and refrigerated. As soon as the house was sufficiently warmed up, they congregated nude in the living room where they began to demonstrate their love for one another in a most physical manner. Not until each one of them expressed their love to every other one of them, and not until everyone had been allowed to spew their juices in some one's mouth or ass, did they retire as couples to their bedrooms. The doors here were always left open.

In the morning, Paul gave Doug a tour of the kitchen. He explained that between March and October they could buy groceries at Fisher's General Store, but in the winter they had to buy their groceries at a Walmart which was up the road near the hospital. "In fact," he said, "we practically have nothing in the house so let's go shopping and we'll eat breakfast out."

They got in the car and stopped first at Rosie's for breakfast. This was a great opportunity to test thing out. He introduced Doug to Rosie as his partner. Rosie didn't seem shocked at all. She gave out a stifled scream, grabbed Paul in a bear hug and told him how happy she was for him. Then she did the same to Doug and welcomed him to Lake Henry. Breakfast was on Rosie that morning. Paul could only hope that Sunday went as well.

They did their shopping and returned home. Paul's fridge had always been close to empty. Now they had to rearrange the shelves several times before they had room for everything. Once everything was in place, he called Randy and he asked if he could come over with Doug to introduce him.

"Absolutely," Randy said. Paul figured that Randy thought that they were coming over so that Randy could meet his new employee, but he was determined to be candid with him and Michelle as well. He wasn't sure how much Liz would understand. He did know she was fond of all the crew, and accepted their relationships without question. She considered every one of them to be an uncle.

Doug was unprepared for the sheer size of Randy. "Somebody should have warned me," he said as he shook Randy's hand and looked up into his eyes. Paul had just said, "This is Doug," when he came in. Now he said, "Randy, Doug is my life partner. He's living with me now."

Randy broke out laughing. "Did you think I didn't know? Uncle Warren and Dan called last night. They didn't say anything at first, but I could tell they were dying to tell me something so I wheedled it out of them. I'm so happy for you Paul, and I know the crew is going to be delighted." He gave Paul a kiss on the cheek, and then he embraced Doug and kissed him too.

Michelle was now doing all of Randy's bookkeeping. She took all of Doug's information that was needed for payroll purposes. Randy told

Doug that he would pick him up Monday morning but that they would not always be working at the same site, and suggested he buy some sort of wheels at the earliest possible opportunity. Michelle offered them coffee, but they declined.

When they got back in the car, Paul said he would like to make one more stop. Doug already knew all about the crew and he knew that Jeff and Jim were the sons of Brian and Tucker, that Michael and Jerry were former college room mates of Jeff and Jim, and that Ron and Foster were the sons of the Fishers whom he would meet on Sunday, the next day.

"I don't want to call them," Paul said. "I'd rather drop in unannounced. This way they'll all be naked and you will see the most beautiful six bodies in the world, except for yours of course," he added laughing. "They might even be having sex. I should say they'll probably be having sex."

Not so. The crew had all slept very late. They had just now finished showering and were in the kitchen preparing a brunch. They were indeed naked.

Paul knocked on the front door which sent them all scurrying. Jeff looked out a window and when he saw it was Paul with some good looking guy, he told everyone that the coast was clear and he let Paul and Doug in.

"I feel so over dressed," Paul said when he saw the naked bodies.

"Then strip already," Jerry retorted.

Instead he put his arm around Doug, kissed him on the cheek and told the guys that they were now partnered. Nobody seemed to be shocked at all. In fact, everyone jumped and shrieked for joy and began hugging and kissing the 'newlyweds' who were bombarded with hard cocks all over their bodies.

"Will you stay for brunch?" Ron asked after all the introductions were made.

They declined, but Ron said, "Well just have a cup of coffee with us and you can tell us all the dirt." That was acceptable. There was not enough room in the kitchen so they opened up some snack tables and ate in the living room.

When Paul told every one how Brian and Tuck had invited him to spend a few days with them in Flagstaff, nobody said anything, but they were all surprised that Brian and Tuck were out to Paul. Jeff determined to ask Paul about that, but he was anxious to hear how they met, so he held his question.

Jim spoke first. "Everyone here has a story to tell that is literally a case of love at first sight." He raised his coffee mug, "Here's to love."

"Here's to love," the others echoed.

"Sometime I'd love to hear all your stories," Doug said. I've already heard about Brian and Tuck.

"At the moment," Jeff said, "I'm more interested in hearing how you came to be invited to a sexual outing with my fathers."

Paul turned beet red, but he told how the fathers had stopped at the Fishers to pick up the key to the country house and he, Warren and Dan were all there for breakfast. Josie insisted, of course, that Brian and Tuck stay for breakfast also. I think your wonderful fathers sensed how lonely I was (glancing at Jeff) and invited me to dinner that night. When I got there I told them about myself and when I told them that I was a widower they expressed condolences at the loss of my wife. That's when I explained to them that everyone assumed that I had lost my wife, but it was my beloved Patrick whom I had lost. I determined then and there to be honest with myself and my community and I'm coming out to everyone tomorrow at services."

Jerry, who already knew, was so proud of Paul. He jumped up and enveloped Paul with his naked body and hugged him tightly. Jerry's prick got harder and Paul's started to erect. It was perfectly noticeable and they all broke out laughing.

"Does this allow Doug and me to come to your nude swim parties this summer," Paul wanted to know.

"Absolutely!" the crew said in one voice.

"Look guys," Paul said as he stood to leave. "I'd like to take Doug to Dave's to look at used cars. He's going to need one for work. So please excuse us." He then looked at them very sternly and in his best ministerial demeanor he said, "And I expect to see every one of you in church tomorrow morning." Then in a very meek and pleading voice he said, "Besides I'll need your support when I come out tomorrow."

"We wouldn't miss it for the world," Michael spoke for them all.

Everyone kissed goodbye and it was such a tangled mess some people got two kisses.

Back in the car, on the way to the used car dealer, Paul could see that Doug was disturbed. "What's wrong, babe?" he asked.

"I've got some money saved," Doug said, "but definitely not enough for a car."

"Doug," Paul said, "listen to me very carefully. I haven't spent any money on myself at all since I came to Lake Henry. I've saved enough for both of us to get new cars, but one will be enough. Just consider it a wedding present. Not only that, but I need a couple of new suits for church and I know you could use some work clothes as well as a Sunday suit. We don't have to spend a fortune. Walmart is open until 10:00 PM. We'll go there after we buy you a car. Please don't fight me on this. I want to do it for us. It's not like you aren't working, and I know you'll do your share when it comes to the household expenses."

Doug leaned over and kissed Paul on the cheek. "How did I get so lucky?" he said to no one in particular. They both distinctly heard someone laugh and Paul knew it was Patrick.

Dave had about fifty used cars on his lot. When he saw that it was his minister getting out of the car, he told himself he'd better give him a very honest deal. If nothing else, Dave was superstitious. Paul introduced Doug to Dave as his partner, and Dave was the first one to express any shock. He didn't say anything but his jaw fell down.

"Are you catching flies," Paul asked him.

"Gee I'm sorry Pastor. I gotta admit you just threw me a fast one. But hey, I love you, so I guess I love Doug here too. All I can say is congrats, and a long and healthy life to both of you. Now what can I do for you?"

They ended up with a three year old Honda Civic. Paul said that they might not be able to pick the car up today and asked how late he was open on Sundays. "We're here until 9 PM today and 6 PM tomorrow," Dave said.

"Please have all the paper work ready as soon as possible. We have some shopping to do at Walmart, and if we can, we'll be back today. If we can't make it, we'll come in tomorrow afternoon."

Dave shook their hands and said the car would be ready for pickup in about two hours. As a special favor to Paul, he said he wanted to service it fully before it left the lot.

Late that evening, Paul and Doug returned home in two separate cars, and fell exhausted on the living room couch. After they recovered, they removed all the tags on their new clothes and hung them away or put them in drawers.

"Too bad the suits needed altering," Paul said. "It would have been nice to have worn them to church tomorrow." Neither was hungry even though they hadn't eaten in hours. Paul made some hot chocolate, which they drank with a couple of slices of toast, and they went to bed. They cuddled for a while and then fell fast asleep, totally exhausted.

CHAPTER TWENTY ONE

Sunday morning dawned to much warmer weather. The sun felt comforting to anyone who was outdoors early in the day. Spring was definitely hiding around the corner.

In the suburbs of Phoenix, Brian and Tucker were getting hard thinking that it would soon be time for their spring fishing trip. Tuck was thinking that now that the crew owned the house, maybe he and Brian could add a day or two to the trip. He would definitely see what he could work out.

In Lake Henry, Paul was in the shower. He was both frightened and excited. Today he was going to introduce his congregation to Doug. So many people already knew that he was gay that he was hoping the rumor had spread. The less shock there was in the church this morning the better.

Doug had already showered and was preparing bacon and eggs in the kitchen. He planned on wearing a sport shirt, slacks and a sport jacket to church. He had laid his clothes out on the bed, and was only wearing a pair of boxer shorts which he had purchased the day before at Walmart. He had also raided Paul's part of the closet and laid out a light suit, shirt, tie, socks and underwear. He felt the light suit looked appropriate for the premature spring like weather.

Paul came out of the shower drying himself, and in all his glory.

Doug said, "You've got to stop parading around naked or we will never get anything done around here." He went over to Paul, embraced him with one arm and grabbed his cock with the other. He kissed him and then released him. "Later," he said to Paul and winked at him.

"Better hurry. Breakfast is almost ready," he let Paul know.

Before he left Flagstaff, Doug had called his two sisters and two brothers and given them his new address and telephone number. Just as he got back to the kitchen the phone rang. He hesitated to answer and Paul yelled from the bedroom, "It's OK to answer the phone. You live here you know."

Doug picked up the phone and barely whispered, "Hello."

"Doug is that you?" his sister Edie asked.

"Hi darling," Doug responded. They spoke for two or three minutes and Doug explained that his partner was a minister and they had to get ready for church so he had to get off the phone. To which Edie chided him that the church would probably be struck by lightening this morning. As soon as he hung up, the phone rang again. This time it was his sister, Ellie. They had a similar conversation. Just as he hung up, Paul came into the kitchen. Doug wanted to cry again. Paul was so dazzling handsome.

Before he could ask, Doug told Paul that his two sisters had called to wish him a happy birthday, but he would be shocked if his brothers remembered to call.

"Oh, sweetheart," Paul moaned, "we've got to really learn more about each other. If only I had known it was your birthday, I would have planned something. I didn't even get you a gift."

"I got a gift from you, sweetheart," Paul answered. "The gift is you, and if that's not enough, which it is, you bought me clothes and a car. That's beyond the call of duty for any birthday gift."

"Don't make me cry while I'm wearing my Sunday best," Paul said as he embraced Doug.

Paul wanted to arrive early at the church, and go to his office in the rear of the church. The day was so beautiful he knew that his flock would all be socializing outside before the service. He didn't want to introduce Doug until he said something in the church. He went around to the back of the church. He sat Doug in a front pew, and he went to his office to wait it out.

Fortunately everybody was so busy talking and socializing they really didn't notice that Paul was not among them. As it got close to starting the service, they all began to mosey into the church and find seats. Liz decided that she wanted to sit with her Uncle Michael and he gladly obliged her, leaving Randy and Michelle sitting with Warren and Dan.

As usual the organist entered and took her place first. She was followed by the choir and then Pastor Paul. Everyone in the church had one of two thoughts when they saw him. Some thought he looked radiant this morning and the others thought he looked exceptionally handsome this morning. Doug thought that he looked like an angel.

The choir led the congregants in a lovely hymn. Everyone had a feeling something was afoot and waited expectantly for Paul to begin his service. He started with the repetitive Sunday ritual of responsive reading. Most of the assembled read the words without giving them much thought, and Paul could tell there was no passion in the reading. He was used to it.

His sermon this day was about falling in love at first sight. The crew, Dan, Warren, Jason and Josie, of course Doug, and a good many other church members, sat up at attention. They had been there and done that and wanted to hear what Paul had to say.

His lesson was from the Old Testament. He related the story of Jacob at the well. He lovingly described Rachel's outer and inner beauty, and how Jacob was smitten at first sight. He went on to explain that poor Jacob had to work for his father in law for many years before he could claim Rachel.

"In today's world," he went on, "we fall instantly in love, marry and then we have to work for our happiness after the wedding. We must never take love for granted," he continued. "Work hard for love. It's worth every obstacle you have to hurdle."

Couples throughout the church took each other's hands and squeezed it. Michael squeezed Jerry's hand with his own left hand and Liz's with his right hand. Doug just sat and cried.

The moment was fast approaching, and in a trembling voice, Paul asked his flock to join him in the social hall after services. Today's libation was to be sponsored by him in celebration of his union to Douglas Jones. He motioned to Doug to stand. For a horrifying few seconds there was utter silence in the church. Then Michael stood up and began to applaud. Immediately, half the congregation joined him. Finally little by little everyone in the church was standing, applauding and cheering.

Paul left the pulpit, took Doug's arm and marched him to the rear of the church. As the congregation piled out, they all stopped to wish the couple well, and Paul introduced Doug to everyone by name. Doug was much impressed.

Paul anticipated a heavier than usual attendance at the social hour and like Jerry, he had arranged for Rosie to handle it all for him. Everyone crowded around Doug for the opportunity to speak to this handsome guy the pastor had snared. They all wanted to know what he would be doing, and when he told them that he would be working for Randy, they were all delighted. He was truly a member of the Lake Henry family.

At one point, Randy had an opportunity to speak to Doug. He just wanted to let Doug know that in addition to industrial construction which was expanding daily in this area of Arizona, he had over a dozen contracts to build summer homes along the lake for the city slickers who had fallen in love with this little town. He assured Doug that his future was secure. Then he whispered in Doug's ear, "Now this is a secret. I got a call from Brian and Tuck. They are a couple of years away from retirement, and they bought a big lakefront lot about a quarter of a mile from the crew. They want me to build two small bungalows where they intend to retire. I'll show you the lot tomorrow. Foster has already designed the houses for me so that they will both be on the lake, but he has no idea who they are for. It's a surprise, so keep it mum."

At that moment, Liz, who was holding Randy's hand, tugged on Doug's pants and asked him if he was going to be her uncle too.

"I guess so," he replied and visions of more Christmas gifts danced in her head.

Little by little, the social hall emptied out and Rosie's crew began their cleanup. She came over to Paul and Doug and gave them each a kiss. Why don't you two go home and enjoy the day. I have the key to the church and I'll secure the building before I leave.

They had no sooner gotten into Paul's car when his cell phone rang. It was Jeff.

"It's such a beautiful spring like day," he said. "We'd like to break in our new deck so we're making a barbeque. Please join us at about 1 PM."

"Wonderful," Paul said. "What can we bring?"

"There's never enough beer at these barbeques. If you have any at home, bring it along, but don't buy special."

Paul and Doug had enough time to change to more casual attire, but before they got dressed again, they celebrated their union in their own special way. As he came in Paul's mouth, Doug said, "Thank you Paul. I love you. I'll always love you. I swear we are for life." Paul started to cry and almost choked on Doug's cum.

There was quite a crowd at the barbeque. Besides the crew, Doug and Paul, there was Randy, Liz, Dan, Warren, and Jason and Josie Fisher. Everyone kept toasting Paul and Doug, and the beer was going fast. Jason had brought some wine so that started to go next. Only Jeff refrained from drinking. He had drawn the short straw and was the designated driver back to

Phoenix. Although the logic escaped him, he was also appointed chief chef at the barbeque because he couldn't drink anyway.

Paul and Doug got two more surprises before the party was over. First Rosie joined them with a big cake which read "Love Always." Then the phone rang and Jerry answered it. He called Paul into the kitchen where it was a little quieter and told him that Brian and Tuck were on the line and wanted to talk to him. They were on separate phones so he could talk to both of them at the same time. Tuck said that his sons had reported fully what happened at the church that morning. He and Brian were overjoyed, but they expected nothing less from the fine people of Lake Henry. Then Brian wished them a long life of love and happiness before they hung up.

When they returned to the deck, Randy asked for everyone's attention. "I have an announcement to make," he yelled as loud as he could. "Liz is going to be a big sister." After that nobody could hear themselves think. Michael almost crushed his little sister when he heard the news. Everyone was crying and laughing with joy.

While all this celebration was going on, Paul walked down to the lake. When he reached the calm waters he turned and looked back at the house. He was pleased to see that all of his dearest friends and loved ones were happily partnered in love. He was sure that his own heart would burst from too much happiness. He bowed his head and said a little prayer:

"Thank you God for your greatest gift, the gift of love. You have given each of these fantastic people, just the right person to love, and spend their lives with. Thank you also, Patrick, for being God's emissary and bringing Doug to me through Brian and Tucker They will always be my friends for the rest of my life."

He felt Patrick's kiss on his cheek. When he looked up, Doug was standing beside him. Doug threw his arms around Paul and pulled him close. Tears were streaming down both their cheeks as they tenderly kissed.

ABOUT THE AUTHOR

Hank Brooks was born in Brooklyn, NY and lived most of his adult life in and around the New York City area.

He is very active in SAGE, a senior advocacy group for gay men and women.

He has three children and five grandsons. He is a retired CPA, and now lives with his partner, Leo, in Coconut Creek, Florida.

Hank Brooks is also the author of *An Anthology of Erotica - Gay Love Stories.* Available at Amazon.com, TheNazcaPlainsCorp.com or your local bookstore.

AN ANTHOLOGY OF EROTICA
Gay Love Stories

by HANK BROOKS

BROOKS

AN ANTHOLOGY OF EROTICA: GAY LOVE STORIES

www.ingramcontent.com/pod-product-compliance
Lightning Source LLC
Chambersburg PA
CBHW051127260626
47170CB00005B/1705